CROSSING the LINE

A MACY McVANNEL NOVEL

REBECKA VIGUS

OPEN WINDOW

Livonia, Michigan

ALSO BY REBECKA VIGUS

Macy McVannel Novels

Rivers Edge

Sanctuary

Other Novels

Out of the Flames

Secrets

Target of Vengeance

Non-Fiction

So You Think You Want to Be a Mommy?

Poetry

Only a Start and Beyond

Children's Books

Of Moonbeams and Fairies

Multi-Author Collections

In Creeps the Night

Dedicated to anyone who has ever been bullied.

AUTHOR'S NOTE

Bullying has become an epidemic in our society. It is time we took it seriously. While this book deals with bullying when it has crossed into a legal issue there are statistics to back up the fact that bullying affects our children adversely and leads them to become bullies in some cases. I have sited here some statistics for you with commentary. I will not give you the entire article but will point you to where you can find it.

- It is estimated that 160,000 children miss school every day due to fear of attack or intimidation by other students.

- 1 in 7 students in Grades K-12 is either a bully or a victim of bullying.

- 56 percent of students have personally witnessed some type of bullying at school.

- 15 percent of all school absenteeism is directly related to fears of being bullied at school.

- 71 percent of students report incidents of bullying as a problem at their school.

- 90 percent of fourth through eighth graders report being victims of bullying.

- Bullying statistics say revenge is the strongest motivation for school shootings.

- 87 percent of students said shootings are motivated by a desire to "get back at those who have hurt them."

- 86 percent of students said, "other kids picking on them, making fun of them or bullying them" causes teenagers to turn to lethal violence in the schools.

- 61 percent of students said students shoot others because they have been victims of physical abuse at home.

- 54 percent of students said witnessing physical abuse at home can lead to violence in school.

- According to bullying statistics, 1 out of every 10 students who drops out of school does so because of repeated bullying.*

*National statistics on bullying in schools, Feb. 14, 2012 by Ofelia Garcia Hunter

The source is the National Education Association Website:

http://www.alicetx.com/news/article_87be339a-5658-11e1-a087-0019bb2963f4.html

The statistics on bullying and suicide are alarming:

- Suicide is the third leading cause of death among young people, resulting in about 4,400 deaths per year, according to the CDC. For every suicide among young people, there are at least 100 suicide attempts. Over 14 percent of high school students have considered suicide, and almost 7 percent have attempted it.

- Bully victims are between 2 to 9 times more likely to consider suicide than non-victims, according to studies by Yale University

- A study in Britain found that at least half of suicides among young people are related to bullying

- 10 to 14 year old girls may be at even higher risk for suicide, according to the study above

- According to statistics reported by ABC News, nearly 30 percent of students are either bullies or victims of bullying, and 160,000 kids stay home from school every day because of fear of bullying

- Bully-related suicide can be connected to any type of bullying, including physical bullying, emotional bullying, cyberbullying, and sexting, or circulating suggestive or nude photos or messages about a person.

- Some schools or regions have more serious problems with bullying and suicide related to bullying. This may be due to an excessive problem with bullying at the school. It could also be related to the tendency of students who are exposed to suicide to consider suicide themselves. **

** Excerpt from: Bullying and Suicide article on the following website:

http://www.bullyingstatistics.org/content/bullying-and-suicide.html

Step up. Make your child, grandchild, niece, nephew, godchild, or neighbor aware. Teach them how to cope with the bully. Get involved. Volunteer at the school. Most schools are required by law to have a bullying policy. Know what it is for your school. Follow the chain of command if your child is being bullied. Be part of the solution.

Thank you.
Rebecka Vigus

CROSSING the LINE

CHAPTER ONE

Monday morning

I walked into the police station and headed toward my desk where I found a bouquet of flowers. I am Macy McVannel, a detective sergeant, on the Rivers Edge Police Force. We had apprehended Riley in connection with three murders. I had succumbed to the stress of it all and my captain ordered me to take a week off.

Eli Patterson, a state police officer, injured during the Drew Riley takedown had whisked me away. He would be returning in another week.

Now back to reality and the workload most likely waiting for me. The flowers were no doubt a welcome back gift from one of my friends. I reached for the card and read it.

"I'll be home soon. Eli"

I was touched, moved them to the corner of the desk, and pulled the first file out of my "In" box. It read APPLETON. Opening it, I found the reports previously e-mailed to the captain. I still needed to write up the report from the last day. Taking a deep breath, I booted up my computer and set out to work on the report. I had not done much when a cup of tea appeared at my elbow. I looked up to see my partner, Tom Maxwell, smiling at me.

He sat at his desk facing me and went to work on his "In" box. The captain had given him a week off to spend time with his family after the birth of his new daughter. He and Shannon had two boys and a newborn daughter—Macy Ida-Mae Maxwell. I felt honored they had named her after me and was sure Ida and Sally Mae felt the same. "Where are the pictures? How is my namesake?" I asked grinning widely. Her baptism would be this Sunday, I was looking forward to it, and Eli would be home by then.

Tom smiled saying, "Shannon said you'd ask me about them first. I'll show them to you at lunch."

I began typing my last report so we could finally close the Appleton case. I had to recall the events which took place at the bunkhouse. *I closed my eyes remembering what had happened that day. I was sitting on the floor with the sofa at my back watching the outside action on TV, JJ Waxman and Sally Mae Davis; the two witnesses I was protecting were in the safe room. There were police guards in the front and back of the house guarding the doors. Riley was making his way toward the bunkhouse through the trees.* I felt the tension in my body as I put myself back in moment and typed. Once I finished, I printed out two copies, signed them, and placed one in the file. I took the file and the extra copy and set them in the "In" box for the captain's secretary. No one felt sorry for Riley. He was the kind of officer who made us all look bad. It was good for all of us when we could rid ourselves of a bad cop.

Back at my desk, I found a note in my "In" box to call the ADA (Assistant District Attorney). I decided to make the call while I waited for Tom.

"Assistant District Attorney Stephens' office," the crisp voice answered.

"This is Detective Macy McVannel returning a call."

"Yes, Detective, I'll put Ms. Stephens right on," her voice said sounding very professional.

"Hello, Macy, welcome back. Hope you are all rested up," Sarah Stephens said cheerfully.

"I am. I just turned in my final reports on the Riley case."

"Good, good I'll look for those to come over. It's not why I called though. I need to talk to you on a different matter," she said seriously.

"Okay, what is it?" I asked wondering *where this crisis would take us.*

"Mrs. Watson is in my office. Is there a chance you and Tom can come and meet her?" she asked anxiously.

"I'll grab him and we'll be right there. Can you give me a heads up?" I sensed the tension in her voice and knew this was serious.

She hesitated then said, "This is something you need to hear first person."

"On our way," I disconnected and went looking for Tom who was still in the break room sipping his coffee. "We have a live one."

"Okay, I'm ready," he said setting the cup down in the sink. We headed to the parking lot for our car.

In the car Tom asked, "Are you going to tell me about it?"

"There's nothing to tell, I don't even know what it's about. The ADA said we need to hear it ourselves," I told him still concerned by the tension I had heard in her voice.

"I hate walking in blind," Tom said, obviously curious because we had no idea what we would be facing.

"Me, too."

We parked near the DA's office and entered together. The secretary led us to ADA Stephen's office. When we entered, Ms. Stephens was consoling an upset woman on the sofa. She rose as soon as she sensed our presence.

"Mrs. Watson, this is Detective Sergeant Macy McVannel and her partner Detective Tom Maxwell." She gestured to each of us with her hand.

"How do you do?" Mrs. Watson said as she stood and shook our hands.

Tom motioned for her to sit and turned two chairs to face the sofa. He took out his notebook which meant I would be asking the questions. When we both sat down, Ms. Stephens asked Mrs. Watson to begin.

Mrs. Watson took a deep breath before beginning, "My daughter, Michelle, is lying in the hospital. She overdosed on some medication and they don't know if she will live." She wiped her eyes and gulped for breath.

"What would you like us to do?" I asked *my mind was already angry because a young girl had hurt herself.*

"I want you to find the person who posted a nude photo of her on the Internet and all over the school. It humiliated her to the extent she tried to take her own life," Mrs. Watson sobbed.

"When did this happen?" I asked horrified.

"Last night while I was at my Bible study group she took the pills. I came home, found her, and called 9-1-1." Mrs. Watson began crying again.

"I'm very sorry, Mrs. Watson. Do you have any idea who took the photo?" I asked needing the information yet angry it had happened.

"I wish I knew. These jerks have been terrorizing my daughter since school started. I've met with the principal and the guidance counselor about it however things only seemed to get worse. Someone took a photo of her in the locker room shower after her swim class, sent it out, and finally sent her over the edge." She was indignant despite her tears.

"How old is Michelle?" I asked wondering at the age of the others involved.

"She turned sixteen last month," her mother answered.

Tom started bouncing his leg a sure sign he was uncomfortable. Since we had been through so many investigations our minds began to run through all the people we needed to interview. "Does your daughter have a close friend?" I asked calmly.

"Kara Dawson is her best friend. She might know where the picture came from. If it wasn't for Kara calling me this morning, I would never have known." Her shoulders shook as she sobbed again.

"Mrs. Watson, we'll do all we can to get to the bottom of this," I tried to reassure her.

"Thank you so much. I need to get back to the hospital."

We stood. "Do you have a car?" Tom asked before she could get out the door.

"No, I took the bus down here," she said quietly.

"Macy and I will drop you off at the hospital. We need to talk to her doctor, if it's okay with you."

"I appreciate it, thank you for offering me a ride," she said kindly.

We left the ADA's office and led Mrs. Watson to our car. I helped Mrs. Watson into the back, and Tom drove to the hospital. Mrs. Watson led us to the ICU-Intensive Care Unit-where her daughter lay as a patient. The attending doctor was not on the floor, but the nurse caring for Michelle was. Mrs. Watson introduced us.

"Please tell the officers anything they want to know about Michelle's health," she said before making her way to her daughter's side.

The nurse nodded and led us away from Michelle's room. When we reached the nurses' station, she said, "Michelle took several sleeping pills. We don't know how many were in the bottle. Some were on the floor near her bed, so she didn't take them all. They pumped her stomach in the ER-emergency room- to see if they could get the drugs out of her system. Now we just have to monitor her vitals and hope she wakes up. We ran a tox screen and she didn't consume any alcohol with the medicine. There is every hope she will awaken. It's up to Michelle at this point. It will depend on how much she wants to live."

"Thank you for the information. Are there any members of family here?" Tom asked.

"Michelle's mom has been the only one we've seen. I don't know if there is other family or not," the nurse told us.

Tom nodded, "Thank you again."

"Please call anytime and we'll try to update you."

We turned to leave. Tom whispered to me, "I wonder where the father is? We need to check on the family."

I nodded and we headed to the car. This case was going to be a mess. I hated when kids were involved. This was going to hurt many people. I drove and Tom called to find out what he could about the family and to have Captain Wellington notify the school superintendent we would be going to the high school to look into this. He would also need to let the school know we need to speak with Kara Dawson. The school could notify her parents and have them at the school.

We were almost at the school when Tom's phone chirped. "Maxwell," he answered. "Okay, we will wait."

"What's up?" I asked curiously.

"Captain is sending us with a search warrant for every student computer at the school. He's also sending a couple of computer techs to begin searching. He wants to know if the photo started there."

"This must be some photo," I said.

"I don't want to see it, Macy. I hate when kids do this to each other. Do you know how many kids take their lives over stuff like Facebook, MySpace, and any number of other social networks out there?" Tom wanted to know.

"Too many."

We rode the rest of the way in silence.

CHAPTER TWO

At Rivers Edge High School we went to the main office where the principal was waiting for us. He escorted us down a hall-way to his private office.

"I'm Duncan O'Brian. This is a tragedy for our school. How can I help you?" He was a rotund man of short stature used to placating irate parents. I found his tone irritating rather than comforting.

"I'm Detective Sgt. Macy McVannel and this is my partner Detective Tom Maxwell. We'll need to talk to Kara Dawson. Have her parents been called?" I asked without emotion.

"They're on their way. What else can I do?" he asked with an affected tone.

"Tell us everything you can about Michelle Watson," Tom said curtly.

The three of us took seats—us on the chairs facing his desk and him behind it. This time I took out my notebook, leaving Tom to ask the questions.

Mr. O'Brian opened a manila file he had on his desk. "I don't know her well. She is new this year. Her records indicate she has excellent attendance and exemplary grades. She's not an instigator and keeps to herself. If she had a problem here, I was unaware of it," he said emotionlessly.

"Her mother told us she has talked to you repeatedly about the harassment of her daughter. Did her name come up in conversations with her teachers?" I went into interrogation mode, asking difficult questions showing no emotion.

"Her mother did accost me in the hall one day. I suggested she make an appointment however, I don't recall her coming in. None of her teachers has mentioned anything to me." O'Brian's response was unflappable.

"She didn't stand out and no one could see she was being harassed here? What kind of school is this?" Tom's irate tone, took the principal by surprise.

I knew Tom was thinking of his own children. They would attend school here in the future. I just kept making notes.

"We'll need to talk to her teachers, the guidance counselor, and we have a search warrant for every student computer in this building. Technicians are in the hallway waiting to scour them for the photo taken in an effort to find out who took it and put in on the Internet," I stated clearly and succinctly.

Mr. O'Brian gave an agitated groan, "Hrrumph. I do believe this is highly unorthodox."

"The attempted suicide of a successful young girl is unorthodox. We are conducting a police investigation. If we find this could have been prevented, if you interceded on her behalf, it will be a crime. It seems to me however, there is a lot you don't recall about her," Tom sneered at the man, looking as if he wanted to choke him.

Tom was working very hard at controlling his emotions. This case was going to be hard enough without him seeing it through a parent's eyes. I would have to talk to him when we were done with this man.

Mr. O'Brian stood, "I'll see if I can get her teachers in to speak with you, unless you have more questions for me." He was trying to save face in the wake of a search warrant.

"Good, my partner and I will wait here," I said with as much politeness as I could muster.

Mr. O'Brian stepped from his office and went to talk to the secretary. I looked at Tom. "You need to keep your parental feelings out of this."

"Macy, he had an opportunity to do something and he didn't. It makes me livid when people ignore the things that *are* wrong," Tom said angrily. "It makes them part of the problem."

"Why don't you go out and see if we can put the techs to work?" I suggested thinking Tom needed breathing room.

Tom nodded and left the room. A student led the two techs and Tom to the computer lab. A third tech went the library. Individual rooms having student computers would be the last checked. We instructed *all* of the teachers not to let anyone on the student computers and to shut them down.

When he returned to the office, the guidance counselor was just entering. Mr. O'Brian stopped her on the way in asking, "Mrs. Wharton, would you like a union representative with you?"

"No, Mr. O'Brian, I'll be fine. Thank you." She opened the office door and he followed her in.

I stood and held out my hand. "I'm Detective Sgt. Macy McVannel and this is my partner, Detective Tom Maxwell."

"It's nice to meet you, I think," she said nervously.

"We need to know if Michelle Watson came to you about being harassed," I started right in with questions.

"She came in about a week ago very upset and said she was tired of being the brunt of jokes and pranks. Unfortunately, I didn't get everything out of her. Based on the information she shared with me, I gave her the 'if you ignore them, they will stop speech'. I did tell her to come back in a week if it hadn't stopped. It would have been today." She hung her head wiping her eyes with her hands, "I'm so sorry. I didn't see how much distress she was in."

"Did you alert her teachers? Check on her? Observe her in the hallways?" I hammered the guidance counselor with questions as though she was in *The Spanish Inquisition.*

"I'm sorry to say I did not," she actually looked ashamed she had done nothing. "I thought it was just more of the drama between girls we get at this age. High school is an adjustment from middle school. The freshmen are no longer the kids on the top. There is a fair amount of teasing at the beginning of the school year. I'd thought by now most of it had settled down. We've been in session for six weeks."

"Her mother mentioned she spoke to you," I asserted.

"Yes, she called. She wanted to know what steps had been taken in regards to the harassment of her daughter. I told her it was up to her daughter to come and see me if she was being harassed. Which is when Michelle came in," she was becoming defensive now.

"The parent calls, the child comes in, and you do nothing? I'm not sure I understand," Tom said showing concern.

"I got her calmed down and sent her to class. That's my job. If she wanted to talk more all she had to do was come back," Mrs. Wharton was very defensive as though she had been backed into a corner.

"What was the specific issue the day she came to see you?" I demanded.

"Something about girls taking pictures. I didn't know if they'd been taken at school or at some other function after school hours," she said flatly.

"The photo in question was published on the Internet after Michelle came to see you. It's the reason she took the pills. Have you seen or heard about this?" My face was red and I was livid.

"No, I haven't. Am I being accused of something?" Mrs. Wharton asked hesitantly.

"Not yet." Silence filled the room like smoke from a fire.

I felt this counselor had a lot to learn about dealing with children. She had done nothing to prevent Michelle from overdosing. Her doing nothing just added to the problem. Even I knew kids had to trust you or they would not speak with you. Michelle had asked for help and been brushed off. Why would she come back? This woman was obviously part of the problem.

Tom looked at Mrs. Wharton with disgust. "You may go back to your duties, whatever they are."

She stood. It was obvious she was not pleased with the outcome of the interview. At the door she stopped and looked back at us, "I can't read minds. How was I supposed to know?" There was a sad look on her face as she walked briskly away.

"At least, she has a sense she could have done more," Tom said.

One of the techs came rushing into the office and the secretary led him directly to us. "I've got it. This is the photo which was sent out. I have a guy working on what ISP (Internet Service Provider) it came from. We should have a person for you in a few minutes."

The perpetrator took a full frontal photo of Michelle Watson in the girls' shower. No wonder she had been distraught. With a look of disgust on his face, Tom shoved the photo away. I could tell this was not easy for him. The tech left and the Physical Education teacher entered.

"Hello, I'm Mrs. Kelly," she said holding a hand out to each of us.

"Detective Sgt. Macy McVannel and this is my partner, Detective Tom Maxwell. Please have a seat. We have some questions regarding Michelle Watson."

"A terrible tragedy, how can I help?" she asked showing a caring side.

Tom reached for the photo and handed it to her, "Can you tell me when this was taken? Do you have any idea who took it?"

She gasped. "It was taken in the locker room showers. I have no idea who took it or when. We have strict policies about students not taking photos in the locker rooms or rest rooms. Where did you get this?"

"It was posted on the Internet after swim class, I believe. Since it was taken there we'll need a list of the girls who participate," I stated bluntly.

"Of course, I'll get it to you right away. I have it on the computer. I'm terribly sorry. I wasn't aware of this photo. I'm usually in the shower and locker area. It must have been the day I was paged to the athletic office. It was the only time I wasn't there." She explained. "I hope you don't think I condone this?"

"We don't, Mrs. Kelly," I said calmly. "At this time we're trying to find out who took the photo and posted it on the Internet. If you can think of anyone, it would help." I was trying a different tact with her. "Can you tell us how the locker room is set up?"

"I have an idea who could have been behind it. The girls have not been kind to Michelle. I've tried to get to the bottom of the teasing and can't put my finger on it. Michelle is an excellent swimmer and I've been trying to recruit her for the swim team. I thought maybe she was considering it." Mrs. Kelly seemed sincerely concerned for Michelle and upset by the situation. "The locker room opens to lockers and a changing area to the left is the athletic office separated by a door. To the right is the shower area. Once I am behind the door in the athletic office I have no view of either the locker changing area or the showers."

"Can you tell us about the teasing?" Tom asked.

"The girls never do anything overtly, it's all subtle. For instance, her undergarments would end up missing one day and we'd find them in a trash can or soaking wet in the sink. I got her to leave extra clothing with me. She knew I was trying to get to the bottom of it. I wish she'd come to me about this." She shoved the offending photo toward me.

"Thank you, Mrs. Kelly. You've been very helpful. Please get us the list as soon as you can. We're going to need to speak to all of those girls," I said and rose to shake her hand.

After shaking our hands she left the room.

"She's the first person who was at least aware things weren't right. I wonder why she didn't tell anyone?" Tom asked puzzled.

"Maybe she did. We didn't ask her. Let's wait and see what the other teachers have to say," I told him.

"Okay, but so far the principal is in the dark and it seems the counselor didn't really care. Who besides Mrs. Kelly even made an effort?" Tom asked.

"I have no idea," I told him. "It might be a good idea to look at the anti-bullying policy they have in place. Maybe we can give them ideas for tweaking it so it will work."

"You're right, Macy. Sometimes I get ahead of myself. This is just making me sick," he shook his head if trying to shake the image of the photo from his head.

"I know. We'll get to the bottom of this," I said with certainty.

"I expect to and hope Michelle will be all right," he said almost as though making a vow.

I nodded thinking; *She would never be the girl she had been. Kids could be so mean. What had made this girl the target? What had she done to deserve this?*

The P.E. teacher re-entered the office and handed me a print out. "These are all the girls in Michelle's swim class. I highlighted the ones I thought could be involved, but I've not found anything to prove my suspicions. I hope it helps."

"Thank you, Mrs. Kelly. It gives us an idea where to start. Did you ever mention your suspicions to any of the other staff?" Tom asked almost as an afterthought.

"Quite often, there were several of us trying to get it figured out. I tried to enlist the counselor, but didn't see anything to show she was looking into it. Michelle never bothered anyone. At least, not so we could see," she said, sadness reflected in her eyes.

"Thank you again."

She left. Tom was pensive. I doodled on my notes. We had to wait for the next teacher to arrive or the techs to come with an ISP address for us, one which would, hopefully, lead us to the person responsible for this photo.

CHAPTER THREE

om was unhappy with this case. I could see it getting under his skin he was either pacing or agitatedly tapping a pencil on the desk. I had to find away to distract him.

"So, Tom, where are we going for lunch?" I asked innocently.

"What? Oh, lunch. I'd better make a phone call. We might be late. I'll be right back," he pulled out his cell phone as he left the room.

While I did not get any information out of him, I had at least gotten his mind on something else. I hated cases involving kids and bullying these days. Kids did not realize just how mean they were being to one another. I wonder how Michelle ended up on someone's list and how it had gone so out of control.

Tom came back in with a woman in tow.

"Lunch is taken care of; we don't have a thing to worry about. I met Mrs. Dawson waiting outside." He gestured toward the woman. "They are sending for Kara. Mrs. Dawson, this is my partner Detective Sgt. Macy McVannel."

I shook hands with Mrs. Dawson and motioned for her to have a seat. "Thank you for coming so quickly."

"I want to know what happened with Michelle as much as anyone. Plus, I don't want my daughter being the next one," she said in a rush.

"The next one what, Mrs. Dawson?" I pounced on the comment.

"The next one those awful girls target for ridicule."

Just then, Kara Dawson entered the room. She saw her mother and rushed to her side. "Oh, Mom, did you hear about Michelle?" she asked in anguish.

Mrs. Dawson hugged her daughter. "I did, it's why these police officers want to talk to you."

She looked at both Tom and me. It was the first time she realized she was not alone with her mother. "I can't talk to them."

"Why not?" I asked thinking it had something to do with girl drama.

"I don't want to be a target. I'm not a snitch," she said defensively.

"Was Michelle a snitch?" Tom asked.

"No, she made the mistake of dating Chelsie's boyfriend," Kara informed him.

"Who is Chelsie?" I asked. This was a new name for us.

"Chelsie Patton is *the* most popular girl in our class. She's dating the captain of the football team, Matt Alexander. Or at least she was until he asked Michelle out." Kara was absently twisting her long brown hair as she answered.

"How does dating someone get this kind of photo taken?" Tom asked slamming the picture onto the table in front of Kara.

"No one gets to date Chelsie's boyfriend but Chelsie. If you cross her, she will make your life hell," she responded without looking at the picture.

"Do you have any idea who took this?" I demanded having trouble keeping my voice even. I was angry at her reluctance to help her friend.

"A bunch of girls were in the locker room the day it was taken. They were all Chelsie's friends. I don't know for sure who took it." Her big blue eyes looked directly at me as if defying accusation.

"When did it show up on the Internet?" I asked calmly trying to regain my composure.

"Thursday it started showing up on the net and cell phones all over school," Kara said. She looked to her mom for support.

"Kara, tell them everything you know," her mother urged.

"It showed up during fourth hour computer class. The teacher had everyone delete it, but it kept showing up everywhere. Someone printed it and taped it to her locker. Michelle was beside herself. She went home early on Thursday. I tried to call her but she wasn't picking up her phone." Kara started crying softly.

"Did you get this awful thing on your phone," her mother asked.

"I got it sixth hour the day everyone started getting it. I thought it was photoshopped. You know, where you put someone's head on a different body?" she explained.

I had heard of photoshopping, but I never thought I would see kids doing *this* to each other. Michelle's was worse because it was a real time photo.

"Did you know who sent it to you? Is your phone with you now?" Tom asked. His patience with this was situation running thin.

Kara reached into her pocket and pulled out her cell phone. She looked at her mother and slowly handed it to me. I flipped it open and quickly found her photo messages, I looked at Tom and said, "Take down this number." he nodded, as I reeled off a phone number, and wrote it down.

Tom looked at Mrs. Dawson, "I want to thank you for coming in Mrs. Dawson. We have no more questions for Kara at this time but we may have some later. We'd like your permission to keep her phone for a while. It will be returned to her before she goes home today."

"Keep it as long as you like, you may come by the house if you have more questions." She looked at Kara and added, "Kara and I will have much more to discuss tonight."

Kara took a few minutes to pull herself together then headed for her class. Mrs. Dawson stood to leave.

I sent a text message to the number on the phone from Kara's phone. Kara: Cum 2 office. Cops caught sum1.

We walked Mrs. Dawson to the office area and asked the secretary to ask the students who were already there to leave for fifteen minutes or so. The next thing we knew, a young lady came rushing to the office. She stopped in her tracks when she saw Tom and me standing there.

Tom motioned her in. As she entered he said, "I'm Detective Tom Maxwell, will you join my partner, Detective Sgt. Macy McVannel and me in the principal's office please?"

The girl nodded and started toward the office. I looked at the secretary and said, "Please get her parents here now." She nodded and started dialing the phone.

She sat in one of the chairs at the table, her brown eyes curiously taking us in as she tossed her long brown hair over her shoulder. *She knew all the right moves to make us think she was something special. I could see right through her actions. They were the actions of mean girls everywhere.* She glanced at the photo lying there. Amazingly, her face showed no emotion.

I closed the door and we sat across from her. "Your parents will be here shortly. The only question we are going to ask you is your name." I said firmly.

Before she could answer there was a knock at the door. Tom rose to answer it and stepped into the outer office. Both the secretary and tech guy were there. He deferred to the secretary.

"Her parents are both on the way. They don't want her questioned until they arrive. I suspect they will come with a lawyer," she said simply.

He nodded his head and assured her the only information we had asked from her was her name.

"Oh, she's Chelsie Patton," she said and walked away.

The tech informed him they had the ISP address and it led back to one Chelsie Patton. Somehow, he was not surprised, yet doubted she took the photo, as she would not want incriminating evidence on her phone.

"Can you tell me if it originated with her; or did someone else send her the photo?"

"I'll check, I just know a mass mailing was sent out by her," he replied turning to leave.

"Thanks for your help. Let me know when you find out where she got the photo from." He left and Tom walked to the secretary. "I need to have Chelsie's CA60 file-the cumulative academic and attendance file kept on all students by the school system."

The secretary looked to where the principal was standing. He nodded and said, "We are giving them full access. I don't want the building put under martial law for them to get what they want." His snide comment was not lost on Tom.

The secretary handed Tom the file and he returned to the inner office. he sat down and flipped through it. "Well, Chelsie, you look like an intelligent young lady," he said pretending to look at her grades and test scores. Tom handed the file to me.

"What do you know about it?" she asked, her attitude saying more than her words. She was looking down at Tom or at least trying.

I looked at Chelsie over the top of her file. "I know from your file your grades are decent, you are involved in extracurricular activities, and appear to be on a fast track to the college of your choice. What I've also learned from the past few minutes is your attitude is going to trip you up."

She glared at me as if her stare would make me go away. *This was the girl of my nightmares, five foot seven, designer clothing, manicured nails, determined to get whatever she wanted no matter who stood in her way.* Michelle was a casualty on Chelsie's road to the boy of her dreams. I also knew Chelsie did not do her own dirty work, she found someone to do it for her. Someone else took the photo. *That* someone would say nothing unless it would keep Chelsie from getting into trouble. We were going to have a battle on our hands.

The door burst open Mr. and Mrs. Patton shoved in followed by, what I presumed, was their lawyer. Mrs. Patton embraced her daughter, "Honey, are you okay? Did these people question you?"

Chelsie dissolved into tears, "Mom, they have been trying to intimidate me." She hugged her mother to show her fears.

Mr. Patton looked at the scene and turned to Tom, "I gave strict instructions my daughter was not to be questioned until I arrived."

Tom stood, "Your daughter has not been questioned other than asking her name and she didn't give it to us. Please have a seat."

Reluctantly Mr. Patton took a seat on the other side of his daughter and the lawyer sat next to him.

Tom had remained standing. He began with introductions, "I'm Detective Tom Maxwell. This is my partner, Detective Sgt. Macy McVannel. We're looking into some bullying here at the high school which has led to the attempted suicide of a student. This photo has been passed around the school for the past couple of days." Tom handed the photo to Mr. Patton who handed it to his lawyer. Mrs. Patton continued to hold their daughter.

"It has come to our attention," I started, "this photo was mass mailed to students from your daughter's computer at home."

"Preposterous," Mr. Patton shouted.

"Sir, please let Detective McVannel finish," Tom interrupted.

"Our technicians have been working on the school computers all morning to find out where the photo came from. They have traced it back to your daughter's home computer. We're trying to track who sent it to her. We need to know why she sent a mass mailing to five hundred students here at school."

"There is no way my daughter sent this out." Mr. Patton was red faced as he turned to his daughter, "Tell them, Chelsie, let's get this nonsense cleared up."

Chelsie turned tear stained eyes to her father, "Daddy, I don't know anything about this photo."

"There you have it. Someone is trying to frame my daughter. She is the victim here." He stood, "We're done, let's go home."

"Not so fast," I also stood. "We're just beginning this investigation and your daughter is a key. She is either part of the problem or she is a witness. Until she answers our questions, no one is leaving. Now sit back down and be quiet, Mr. Patton."

Mr. Patton's lawyer tapped his arm and he sat. Chelsie looked at her father dumbfounded. I could see her disappointment in her father for allowing us to continue asking questions.

I took my seat and looked at Chelsie, "Now young lady, I need some honest answers from you. Why did you send out this photo?"

She looked at me defiantly, "I did *not* send out that stupid photo."

"Your first lie, Chelsie, we have documentation from the computer techs and I have a cell phone you sent it to. In fact, I sent you the message from the cell phone to come to the office and you came." I was very calm as I talked to her. "Now let's try again. Why did you send this photo?"

"The bitch was trying to steal my boyfriend," she spat the words out.

Her mother gasped, "Chelsie."

"Enough," her father said.

"Like this shocks you," the chip on her shoulder seemed to grow. "She'd been warned to back off."

"Who warned her?" Tom asked quietly.

"My friends all told her Matt was my man. She didn't listen and kept making dates with him. I don't know why she had to throw herself at him. He's not interested in her," Chelsie's petty jealousy showed through.

"So, you thought taking an unauthorized photo and sending it out would stop it?" I was incredulous to think she would carry jealousy this far.

"I didn't take the photo, it was sent to me, by one of my friends. I knew it would put the slut in her place. I hear the reason they moved here is because she had a reputation for doing all the guys and male teachers in her old school." She tossed her hair as if she was justified in driving a girl to suicide.

"Your information couldn't be more wrong. She moved here because her father died and they came home to be with her mother's family, to rebuild a life." I said succinctly. "You set out to destroy a young girl who lost her father over a boy? Who made you the judge and jury?"

Chelsie gasped, "It's not true. I heard from someone reliable."

"It *is* true. Michelle lost her father a few months ago. Her mom was from Rivers Edge and decided to move home after their loss. She sold their house and all their belongings to come here and start over. You may have taken the chance from them both."

"I didn't make her take pills. She took them on her own." Chelsie was still in defiant mode.

"You taunted her, threw her clothing in the showers, made sure her lunches were knocked to the floor, her books knocked out of her arms in the hallway and papers snatched up and later thrown away. She still has managed to get all A's but this, *this* was uncalled for. I want to know from you who took the photo and I want to know NOW." I said leaning across the table toward her.

"I did none of those things. I never even talked to the bi... Michelle," she glared at Tom. "I don't know who sent me the photo."

"Did it come on your computer or your cell phone?" I asked calmly.

"It came to my computer. I don't know who sent it," she said pouting.

"You sent it to your own cell phone," I politely told her.

"You've got to be kidding? Why would I do something so stupid?" she shouted then looked away dismissing me.

"In order to send it to your friends," I said opening Kara's phone to the photo message Chelsie had sent.

"Chelsie," her father said sternly, "I've had enough of your attitude. You are responsible for sending this photo on the Internet and via your phone. You no longer have either. Give me your phone now."

She looked at her father as though he had grown horns then scoffed, "Yeah right, Dad, make a show for the cops. Take my phone now and I'll have it when we get home."

The lawyer spoke for the first time, "No, Miss Chelsie, I will be taking your phone. I'm sure the police have already sent someone to take your computer." He held up his hand to her father. "They will have a legitimate search warrant; there is nothing you can do." He took the phone, as Chelsie continued to sulk, and turned to me, "What charges are you looking at for Miss Patton?"

"At the moment it will be distribution of pornography involving a minor. There may be other charges as the investigation progresses," I responded.

"Thank you. Do you have more questions or are we free to leave?" the lawyer asked.

"I just want to know the name of the person who took the photo. Chelsie giving up the person will look good for her with the judge," I replied.

The lawyer looked at Chelsie, "If you want the judge to look favorably at you, then you had better give the detective a name."

"Sure, I can give her a name, Mickey Mouse," Chelsie chirped looking smug.

"You may take her now, her lack of cooperation has been duly noted," I said, nodding to where Tom was taking notes.

This time Mrs. Patton spoke up, "Chelsie, you are going to a juvenile center. Don't you understand? The more you mock these officers and refuse to cooperate, the longer you will be there. You have done some terrible things."

Chelsie looked at her mother in disgust. "Honestly Mom, you watch way too many TV shows. This is my first offense and it's not serious. I will be given probation. They can't touch me. Besides I'm a Patton of *the* Patton family."

I could hardly suppress a smile at the girl's audacity. Looking at Mr. Patton I said, "You and your wife are free to go. Your lawyer may meet us at the police station where he can represent Chelsie at arraignment. Chelsie, will you stand please Detective Maxwell is going to place you in handcuffs while I read you your rights."

Dumbfounded, Chelsie stood and Tom cuffed her behind her back as I read her the rights provided to her under Miranda. It seemed as though this were just an exercise to her until she heard the cuffs snap. Her whole attitude changed as she looked at her parents and cried real tears this time. "Daddy, please don't let them do this. Mommy, they can't take me out of here like this. What are people going to say? How can you let this happen?"

I scooped up her CA60 and the note pad. Tom led Chelsie out of the office followed by her mother, father, and lawyer. I was the last one out and handed the file to the secretary. Tom and I, with a tearful Chelsie between us, started out of the building. The bell to change classes rang as we stepped into the hallway. Chelsie held her head high, although tears coursed her cheeks, still believing she was invincible as we headed to the car.

It was a quiet ride to the station. Chelsie's fingerprints and mug shots were taken. We turned her over to the officers who led her to the holding cell. She would be the first one arraigned after lunch. It would do the girl some good to sit for a couple of hours with hookers and junkies. She would get a taste of what she was facing. I hoped it would make her more cooperative.

Tom and I stopped at our desks to check in and then headed to lunch. I could see he was in a better mood; the tension creasing his brow earlier was gone. He was giving me this funny smile, which it also meant he had some kind of secret.

CHAPTER FOUR

e took the car and I was surprised to see we were headed toward the Appleton farm. "Tom, are you sure we should just drop in on Ida like this?" I was a bit worried she might not be up to company yet.

"Oh ye of little faith," he said with a goofy smile on his face. At the farm, Tom drove directly to the bunkhouse.

My smile faded as I remembered the last time I had been here. I had fallen apart on the job and pointed my weapon at JJ. I still did not know how he felt about it. I was feeling uncomfortable, as this was now JJ's home.

"This is probably a mistake," I said hesitantly.

"Trust me, Macy," Tom said as he put the car in park and got out.

I reluctantly followed him to the front door. I had hoped to put off returning here for a long while. I did not want to remember the day I became a failure.

Tom opened the door and stepped aside. I walked in completely unprepared for the sight in front of me. A banner hung from the kitchen rafters which read: **WELCOME BACK MACY!** The kitchen itself smelled of baked bread, something sweet, and a dozen other heavenly aromas. In the room were Sally Mae, JJ, Ida, Shannon holding baby Macy, a lady I did not recognize, and Eli, who was not due back for another week. His dark wavy hair just the way I remembered. Those blue eyes like pools I could drown in. Everyone shouted, "SURPRISE!" at the same time.

I was speechless and overwhelmed by the love flowing in the room. This was my family. I loved each and every one of them.

Tom closed the door. Chuckling he said, "So, will this be okay for lunch, Macy?"

I laughed although tears ran down my cheeks. "Oh very much so, it's my favorite place to eat."

"I cleared it with Captain Wellington, we can take a long lunch today," Tom said smugly.

"You had this all planned, but how?" I was still incredulous.

JJ came to the rescue, "Let's get some chow and we'll tell you all about it."

Everyone found a place at the table, Shannon put the baby down and I was introduced to JJ's mom, Angela Waxman. She seemed subdued, probably because she was new to our group. Time had not been kind to her; she looked rundown from years of hard work. She kept her brown eyes down most of the time, however when she smiled it transformed her face into one of beauty.

Lunch was a bit of everything, homemade bread, a pasta salad, several kinds of sandwiches, steamed broccoli, and for dessert, there were chocolate brownies with ice cream and pecan pie. I would have to do a double workout after this.

Everyone helped themselves and the questions started flying all at once. Ida finally held up her hand and said patiently, "Children, we cannot all talk at once." Everyone laughed.

Sally Mae started the ball rolling again. She looked at Eli then me and asked innocently, "Are you two going to tell us about your week away?"

I blushed and caught Eli's eyes, once again feeling as though I could easily get lost in them. He quickly answered, "Not just yet. I think Macy needs to be brought up to speed on what happened here in her absence."

I nodded swallowing my bite of sandwich and replied, "Ida, I'm glad to see you out of the hospital. How are you doing? Are you managing to keep the house up? "

"I am not staying in the house. JJ has moved me into the bunkhouse because it is all contained on one floor. Sally Mae comes every day to keep me company and most days Angela comes with her. Did you know Angela had studied to be a physical thera-pist? She gives me a daily work out and I am getting stronger every day." She beamed at Angela.

I could see the two of them had become fast friends. They were close in age and both understood what it was like to lose a son. At least for Angela, JJ was still alive.

Sally Mae chimed in, "I am working at a local insurance agency as a secretary and am studying to be a real estate agent."

"Wow, Sally Mae, that's great!" I raised an eyebrow as I smiled. There was no end to what this woman would try. She was definitely not the drama queen I initially expected her to be.

Shannon nodded toward the crib. "Macy Ida-Mae keeps our whole family hopping. The boys love her and spoil her like crazy. We have taken to calling her Mimi. She has Tom wrapped around her little finger and has acquired two more grandmothers. Shannon's smile encompassed both Ida and Angela.

I could see they were becoming quite a close-knit group, my family. It was nice to be with them again. I no longer worried JJ hated me for pulling a gun on him.

JJ, as if reading my mind put his hand on mine, "Macy, I knew you wouldn't hurt me. I've become quite a farmer in the past week. I wish I'd done this much hard work as a kid."

"Okay, Macy," Tom interjected, "your turn to tell us about your week."

"Eli whisked me away in a private jet to his family's island compound in the Caribbean. There I awoke and could walk out my door down to the beach. It was just what the doctor ordered. His whole family showed up, including several nieces and nephews. No one asked any questions and I was able to rest."

"Why do I think she is leaving a lot out, Eli?" Tom asked in his interrogator tone.

"She left out the part where my family loves her. My sister, the physical therapist, worked me like a dog so I could be on a plane home right behind Macy. She also didn't tell you she is wonderful with kids," he said smiling at me.

I looked at Eli pretending frustration, "Just how did you manage to get a flight so quickly?"

"I have an in with the pilot he is my brother." He smiled and took my hand.

There it was again, the blush creeping up my neck and into my cheeks. I thought I had gotten over blushing as a teen. I tried to think of some way to divert attention away from me.

"Are we ready for dessert?" I asked starting to rise.

JJ was up before I could completely rise, "You sit back down, I have it under control." Sally Mae cut the brownies and put them on plates ahead of time; all he had to do was add the vanilla ice cream. Sally Mae got up to serve. Conversation temporarily halted as we ate our desserts.

"Eli," Tom nodded in his direction, "do you need a place to bunk this week?"

"I haven't gotten around to it. JJ picked me up at the airport this morning and we came right here. I know I can't go back to my place, I can't do the stairs. The leg is not ready yet."

"I'll swing by after work and pick you up," I said nonchalantly, "We can figure something out then." I glanced around the table to see meaningful looks pass between Sally Mae, Shannon, JJ, and

Tom. I put my head down and concentrated on my dessert as I felt the blush beginning again.

"Sure thing, Macy, I can work with Mrs. Appleton on physical therapy," Eli said trying to make me feel less embarrassed at the way the conversation had been going. He reached for my hand under the table and gave it a squeeze.

"Well, it's settled except for one thing," Ida declared. "If we are going to do physical therapy together young man, you will call me Ida." She chuckled at Eli's chagrin. "I think since you and JJ got me safely to the ambulance and then you were shot afterward we are beyond the Mrs. Appleton stage."

"Thank you, Ida," he replied with a smile.

Lunch was over all too soon. Sally Mae, Angela, and Shannon cleaned up the lunch dishes. I was able to hold my goddaughter and feed her a bottle. Then Tom and I headed to the door. Eli followed behind us, as I turned to confirm I would pick him up after work, he planted a quick kiss on my cheek. I left quickly before anyone could say anything.

We rode in silence for a few minutes before Tom finally said, "Is this thing with Eli going to get serious?"

I looked at him questioningly, "Have you become my big brother now?"

"Nope, just want to know where your head is."

"Here's the thing, when we're on the case, then my head is on the case," I retorted defensively. "When I am off duty my head will be where it needs to be. As far as Eli goes, I don't know."

Tom looked at me quizzically, "Good enough for now."

CHAPTER FIVE

Back in the squad room, Tom and I checked in then headed for the courthouse. We both wanted to be on hand to see the arraignment of Chelsie Patton. I was personally hoping she would have to spend the night at a juvenile detention center.

Inside, the courtroom was quiet. The aging wood gave it an atmosphere of reverence. The judge had not yet called the case. I could see Mr. and Mrs. Patton sitting behind their lawyer. Mrs. Patton had been crying and was twisting a white hankie in her hand. Mr. Patton leaned forward and whispered earnestly to the lawyer. He did not appear to like the answers he was getting. Chelsie sat ramrod straight staring at the judge's bench as if she were a world away from all of this.

The bailiff asked us to all rise, as the judge entered and took her seat. I was surprised to see Judge Elizabeth Allen was presiding over the case today. I thought she had taken a leave for personal reasons, but I must have been wrong. Elizabeth Allen was not known to take pity on the people who came before her. She was a small, pudgy woman, with gray hair worn in a French twist. She believed everyone should have had a good upbringing and learned the word of God.

She brooked no nonsense in her courtroom. This was going to be very interesting.

The bailiff called the case against Chelsie Patton. She was charged with one count of distributing pornography, one count of trafficking pornography of a minor via the Internet and cell phone, one count of defamation of character, and one count of malicious mischief. Judge Allen looked out at the girl in front of her and asked, "How do you plead?"

Chelsie gave the judge a surly look and said, "Not guilty."

I wondered if her parents had impressed on her the necessity of behaving in the courtroom.

"Young lady, do you understand the severity of the charges against you?" the judge asked.

"Yeah, I guess." Chelsie rolled her eyes as if she was bored and her tone implied she was.

Judge Allen replied, "The correct response is 'yes' or 'yes, your honor.' "

Chelsie glared at the judge. I could tell she was barely concealing her dislike of the court process. I expected fireworks soon.

"Prosecution on bail," the judge said looking at the District Attorney.

"Your honor, a young girl is lying in a coma as a result of the defendant's actions. We are recommending the maximum, $50,000."

I could hear Mrs. Patton sobbing into her hankie. Mr. Patton had sucked in his breath. Before the Patton lawyer could say a word, Chelsie spat, "What the hell for? I didn't commit a crime."

"Young lady, hold your tongue. There will be no swearing in my courtroom. You most certainly did commit crimes. Several, and we'll deal with each one of them." The firm rebuke from the judge did not sit well with Chelsie.

"I am inclined to go along with the District Attorney; however, I think there are other things beyond money at play here. First, I am not sure the young lady understands the extent of her part in this. So, this is what we are going to do." She looked directly at Chelsie then continued, "You *will* surrender your cell phone to the District Attorney. Nor will you be allowed to use any electronic device for communicating to anyone. You have a ten o'clock curfew every night and will wear an ankle monitor. Your parents will still need $25,000 in bail, money which *will* be set aside for victim support."

Chelsie exploded, "What the hell?! I haven't done anything wrong! You're just trying to make some stupid point. It's not my fault the loser girl couldn't take a little joke."

Her lawyer tugged on her arm and whispered in her ear. He was trying to get her to shut up. She was turning red in the face from her anger as she tried to brush him off her.

The judge banged her gavel. Silence reigned for a moment. "Young lady, you need to learn some decorum. In the meantime, until you can be fitted with a monitor, you will be housed in the Rivers Edge Juvenile Center overnight. We're done here." And the gavel came down again.

Court officers came to remove Chelsie. She swung her arms, screaming, "Get off me! Let go of me!"

Judge Allen was at her limit with Chelsie, "Restrain *that* young woman, now!"

Two court officers and the bailiff got her subdued and in handcuffs. She was then led away to be transported to Rivers Edge Juvenile Center. I was silently applauding the judge; Chelsie was going to get a taste of her own medicine.

Tom and I rose and left the courtroom. We still had more students to interview. As much as I wished we were done with Chelsie, this was only the start. We had to find out who took the photos. I thought this was just the beginning but a foreboding feeling came over me.

CHAPTER SIX

Tom and I walked silently back to the station. He headed for the break room to indulge in coffee. I went to make a list of students we still needed to interview. I would take the lead on how we would to proceed. There was more here than what we knew, I felt it.

"Hey, Macy," I turned at the sound of Captain Wellington's rich baritone voice, "Do you have a minute?"

I rose and walked toward his office. He closed the door and indicated I should take a seat. He settled behind his desk before asking me, "How are you feeling?"

"I'm fine, Sir." My tone was noncommittal because I needed to know where he was coming from. I did not think I had screwed up today.

"Did the week off help you get rested and get your head back in place?" His question seemed friendly enough.

"It did and I'm glad to be back at work," I replied honestly.

"You and Maxwell caught a case?" He inquired.

"Nothing we can't handle. It's a case of bullying which crossed the line," I answered.

"Keep me in the loop. If you need anything, give a holler. Good to have you back." I was dismissed. I stood, left his office, and returned to my desk. Tom, who was now sitting at his desk, glanced up with a questioning look.

"I'm fine. The captain just wanted to welcome me back," I said brushing off his concern. "I have a list of some of the kids we need to talk to."

"LET'S GET THEIR addresses from the school and talk to them at home. If we hit their homes around dinner time we should get at least one parent," he said more to himself than to me.

"You want to call the school or shall I?" Anticipating his response, I reached for the phone.

"Neither one, I want to go to there. I want those kids to wonder who is next. They need to feel our presence," Tom was quick to say.

I sat the phone back in its cradle and grabbed my notepad. "Let's roll, then."

As we headed back to the high school I mulled over Tom's perspective about us being a presence. Too bad, we could not be a daily presence in the school. Maybe the bullying could be stopped before it got out of hand. I glanced at Tom trying to read his face, but the effort was for naught.

When we arrived at the school, Mr. O'Brian met us at the door. He looked displeased to see us in his building again. "What can I do for you now, *officers?*" he snapped impatiently.

"We need addresses and parent contacts for a list of students. We will not be questioning anyone else here today," I replied politely.

"I don't think I can just give you the information," O'Brian blubbered.

"I can have Detective Maxwell call the Superintendent's office to find out if you'd like." I replied confidently. I was not taking anything from this man.

He sighed, "No need, I'll have my secretary assist you." He turned to walk into the office. We followed him.

"Mrs. Sweeny," he directed his attention to the secretary. "Please give these *officers* the information they need." He continued on to his office and closed the door.

Mrs. Sweeny, who had been so helpful when we visited the school previously, rose from her desk, and came to the counter to see what it was we needed.

"I'll leave you to this, Macy," Tom said quietly. Then he turned and walked into the hallway.

Right then it sunk in *he* was going to wander the halls and be the "presence" in the building today. I chuckled to myself as I opened my notebook and handed it to her.

"I'll need the addresses and parents' names for these students," I said to Mrs. Sweeny.

She took my list and headed for her desk. Then she pulled up a screen on her computer, and pushed a couple of buttons. Immediately the printer began to spit out information. I was amazed at how easy this turned out to be. As soon as it stopped printing, Mrs. Sweeny brought the papers to me and asked, "Is there anything I can help you with, Detective McVannel?"

"Yes. In fact, there is. Do you have any idea who might be best friends with Chelsie Patton?"

She paused for a minute then reached for the papers she had just handed me. I gave them back to her. She flipped through them and pulled two. "These are the two girls she spends the most time with." She put the two papers on top and handed them back. "Personally I think they are all brats. They have this "better-than-everyone" attitude."

I thanked her just as the bell rang to dismiss the students. Then I stepped into the hallway looking for Tom. I knew he would be there somewhere because he would want the kids to know he was watching. I decided to watch, too. I did not know if being there would make a difference, but I was looking for things out of the ordinary. Or maybe I was looking for the ordinary, these were teenagers after all.

Then it dawned on me. The normal pushing, shoving, playful punching, laughter, and excessive chatter which typically happened at the end of the day were missing. The students went out of their way to appear invisible. This was the difference my presence in the hall made. Those kids, normally tormented on the way to busses or cars, were left alone. This is the impact Tom was hoping to have. I started looking over the kids down the hall to see if I could spot anything going on at lockers. I saw Tom making his way toward the office area. He stopped to chat with a couple of boys. I smiled thinking Tom looked much more relaxed than on our first visit.

He joined me, high fived a young boy and we walked to the car together. All the time I was scanning the area for any sign of trouble. Fortunately, there was none.

In the car, Tom turned to me and asked, "What did you learn?"

I pulled the papers out of my notebook and held up the two on top. "Mrs. Sweeny says these two are chummy with Chelsie and have uppity attitudes. I also have the address for Chelsie's boyfriend. Where do you want to start?"

"Let's start with the boyfriend, his name again?" Tom replied starting the car.

"Matt Alexander. His address is 225 Maple Avenue. Parents are Bradley and Kristen," I replied reading from the paper Mrs. Sweeny had given me.

"Tom, I want to talk strategy," I started. "I need to take the lead on this interview."

"Sure, what are you hoping we can find?" he asked curious to learn what I was thinking.

"For one thing, was Chelsie really his girlfriend? It would be nice to know if he had any idea this photo was going to circulate before it did," I replied matter-of-factly. "I just don't get a feel for his role in this."

"Maybe he doesn't have a role and is just as much a victim as Michelle," Tom said thoughtfully. "Girls have been known to do stupid things to get a guy's attention."

"That's one of the scariest things I've heard today. I don't see Chelsie as doing this alone and I want to bring down this little ring of terrorists at the school. No one should go through the day in fear of humiliation," I said adamantly.

"We should call the Alexander's," he suggested. "It might be a good idea to know if the parents are home."

"Probably, I'll make the call?" I answered as he drove.

I pulled out my cell phone and dialed the number listed for the Alexander's. A woman answered almost immediately, "Hello?"

"Is this Mrs. Alexander?"

"Yes."

"Mrs. Alexander. This is Detective Sgt. Macy McVannel, my partner and I would like to talk to you, your husband, and your son, Matt. Would now be a good time?" I responded. I wondered what was going through her mind as I waited for her answer.

"Um, my husband isn't home yet and Matt has football practice. Can I ask what this is about?" She sounded confused.

"It would be better if we could talk to the three of you at once. The sooner we talk, the sooner we can get this matter all cleared up," I told her.

"If you can give us half an hour, I'll call my husband and have him pick Matt up on the way home," She sounded more in control.

"Half an hour will be just fine, we'll be there," I said and disconnected.

"What's your read on the mother?" Tom asked.

"We caught her off guard, but she recovered quickly. I'm willing to bet she is on the phone with her husband as we speak," I replied.

Tom turned and we stopped at the drive-through coffee shop. After we purchased our beverages, we drove to the Alexander residence. Since we had some time to kill, we sat in the car across the street drinking our coffee and looking at the other addresses and photos we had been given.

In less than fifteen minutes, a car pulled into the Alexander's driveway. Matt slammed out of the passenger side still in his practice uniform. Mr. Alexander was yelling, "What do you mean you don't know what you did? How can you not know why the police want to question you? Don't you walk away from me!" He yelled as Matt ignored him and continued into the house.

It had been an interesting exchange. We still had fifteen minutes before we were scheduled to arrive. Having seen enough, Tom started the car and drove us to the neighborhood park down the street. We finished our coffees in silence.

CHAPTER SEVEN

We arrived at the Alexander house exactly thirty minutes from the time I made the initial phone call. Mrs. Alexander answered the door, a trim woman with dark brown hair worn in a loose curl style to her shoulders. Her outfit was a chic navy blue suit with a cream silk blouse under it. She led us into a formal living room where her husband paced and her son looked uncomfortable. Mr. Alexander was in a dark grey business suit, white shirt, and pale blue tie. Matt had showered and changed into jeans and a T-shirt.

"Won't you please sit down," Mrs. Alexander said in her best hostess voice. "Can I bring you something to drink?"

"No, thank you," I replied as I took a seat near Matt. "I'm Detective Sgt. Macy McVannel and this is my partner, Detective Tom Maxwell."

"What has my son done?" Mr. Alexander asked cutting to the chase.

I looked at him before answering, "I don't know if your son has done anything. Won't you please join your wife?" I indicated he should sit on the sofa next to his wife.

Tom had a clean sheet in my notebook ready for taking notes. I looked at Matt and asked, "Do you know a girl named Michelle Watson?"

"Has the girl accused my son of something?" Mr. Alexander demanded. "What has she said he's done?"

"Mr. Alexander, please," I said calmly then turned to Matt again, "Do you know her?"

Matt nodded affirmatively and said, "We have gone out a couple of times. She was tutoring me in geometry."

"Were you aware some other girls had been picking on her because she went out with you?" I continued.

"Not until today," he replied hanging his head.

"What exactly is going on?" Mr. Alexander began.

"Michelle Watson is in a coma at Rivers Edge Medical Center, Mr. Alexander, we are talking to people who know her," I said, "Would you please just let your son answer. He is not accused of anything."

Mrs. Alexander gasped, "Will she be okay?"

I looked at her, "At this time, the doctors do not know." I opened the file I had and took out the photo of Michelle, handed it to Matt, and asked, "Did you get a copy of this?"

He barely looked at the photo and said, "Yeah, two days ago. I deleted it. I thought it was photoshopped."

"Do you know who took it?" I asked.

He handed the picture back to me and replied, "No, but I wish I did. I'd take them out and beat them."

"Matt," his mother said a look of horror on her face, "why would you say such a thing?"

"Mom, Michelle and her mom moved here because her dad died. She's smart, funny, and pretty. She helped me in geometry so I could keep my grades up. I like her and asked her out. I didn't know anyone was going to hurt her because she liked me," he shook his head, "This is my fault. I should have left her alone."

"What exactly happened to this young woman?" Mr. Alexander asked. "And what is the picture you showed my son?"

I handed him the picture. Mrs. Alexander gasped. Mr. Alexander looked like he was going to tear it up, thought better of it, and handed it to me. Then he said, "I still haven't heard what happened to put her in the hospital."

"She saw this photo and knew it had been sent to hundreds of students in the school and attempted to take her own life. Her mother found her and called for an ambulance. They pumped her stomach in the ER but she has not yet regained consciousness. We are talking to people who know her, trying to piece all of this together."

"Can she have visitors?" Matt asked hopefully.

"It makes no difference, you will be staying away from her," his father answered sternly.

"Yes, she can," I replied quietly.

Matt looked at me with a 'thank you' expression on his face.

"When did you know there was a problem?" I asked him.

"Thursday, everyone got *that* stupid photo. I tried to talk to Michelle, but she said she was sick. I told her to wait until lunch and I'd take her home. She did and I took her home. I really thought someone had done some photoshopping on it. I didn't know it was Michelle. I would never have left her alone. I got worried when she didn't show up on Friday. I tried calling her and texting her all day," he said earnestly. "If I hadn't taken her home, do you think this could have been prevented?"

"I don't think so. Did you get any response from her on Friday?" I asked. I was feeling very sorry for this kid and the worst questions were still to come.

"Yeah, I got a couple of texts in the morning saying she was still sick. At lunch, she picked up but we didn't talk long. Then I didn't hear anything else," Matt replied he was wringing his hands.

"Had you been dating Chelsie Patton?" the question just seemed to come out.

"NO! She's been chasing me for three years. I'm not interested in her," he nearly shouted.

"Did you ever date Chelsie?" I asked.

"No, I did dance with her one time three years ago when we were in junior high. Now she tries to get in my space all the time. She's too stuck on herself for me," Matt said dully.

"Did you know she was behind the photo?" I asked.

Matt looked up; shock written on his face, "NO WAY!"

"I'm sorry to say, she was the one who sent the e-mailed photo. We are still trying to find out who took the picture and who sent the text photos. Do you have any ideas?" I continued probing.

"How could she, why did she, oh, man," Matt started in disbelief. "I don't know, but if I had to guess it would be her two best friends, Abby Stark and Katelyn Walker."

I could see Tom writing the names down. We had what we came for; it was time to wrap this up.

"Mr. and Mrs. Alexander, I want to thank you for your time. Matt, you've been a big help," I said as Tom and I rose. "We can see ourselves out." We walked to the front door.

Behind us, Mrs. Alexander sobbed, "How could those girls do this?"

"I don't want you mixed up in this anymore, Matt," Mr. Alexander demanded.

Outside as Tom and I walked toward the car, he said, "I feel bad for the kid. He's caught up in something not even of his making."

"I suspect he and his mom will find a way to help Michelle and her mom," I responded.

"It would be nice," Tom replied, "I don't see Mrs. Alexander doing much against her husband. Matt could be a different story."

"Where to next?" I asked as we got into the car.

"Well, Abby Stark was the first name he gave us and the top one from Mrs. Sweeny. Let's start there, but I don't want to call ahead," Tom said.

"Sounds good to me," I said as I gave him an address.

CHAPTER EIGHT

It didn't take us long to reach an area of older homes. Most had been well taken care of preserving the Victorian era which once marked the entire town. The Stark home was in the middle of the block and well maintained. Tom pulled the car into the driveway and we approached the house. He rang the bell and we waited for someone to come to the door. I think we were both surprised to see Abby open the door.

Her appearance was one of super model hopeful, clothing very hip and expensive. She was probably five feet seven inches without the platform shoes. A colorful headband held back her long blonde hair which hung almost to her waist. She gave us the once over and turned to yell, "Mom, Dad, it's for you." Then she promptly walked away leaving us standing at the open door.

Mrs. Stark was a lovely woman. I could see where Abby got her looks from. While her mother was tall and thin, she wore her clothing in a casual way. It was easy to see money was not spared when it came to wardrobe, manicures, and jewelry for Mrs. Stark.

"Yes, how may I help you?" she asked.

"I'm Detective Sgt. Macy McVannel and this is my partner Detective Tom Maxwell. We need to talk to your daughter, Abby and we'd like you and your husband present if possible," I replied in my professional voice.

She nodded and motioned us in. We followed her into a living room. Mr. Stark was reading the newspaper and the TV was on to the news. Two younger children were playing a game at a table in one corner. "Kids, take the game up to your room," Mrs. Stark said as she entered. She picked up the remote and turned off the TV. "Gavin, we need to talk with these two police officers."

Mr. Stark put his paper down and slowly rose. He stretched out his hand as I did the introductions again. Then he walked to the hallway and bellowed, "Abby, get your butt down here now!"

He returned to his seat. Within minutes, we heard Abby clunking down the stairs.

"Yeah, Dad?" she asked as she flounced into the room. She stopped surprised we were still there.

"Have a seat young lady, these police officers have some questions for you," he ordered.

She dropped into the nearest chair and pretended to study her nails.

"Abby, how well do you know Michelle Watson," I asked quietly.

"Is she like the girl who tried to kill herself?" Abby asked.

"She is. How well do you know her?" I repeated the question.

"I don't," she replied and flipped her hair over her shoulder.

"Can you tell me anything about this?" I asked handing the photo to Abby.

"A bunch of people at school got this," she said without looking and handed it back.

Her mother reached for the photo. Tom handed it to her. She gasped. "What do you mean a bunch of you got this? Who is this? Why did you get it? Who sent it?" She shoved the photo toward her husband.

"Geez, Mom, it's no big deal. Someone took a picture in the shower. What's the problem?" Abby was bordering on insolent.

"The problem is a young girl tried to take her life because of this photo. It's illegal to take such photos and illegal to send them," I explained. "Now I need you to sit up, pay attention, and answer my questions."

Abby looked at me as if I was an alien. "She's new this year. I don't know her. She's in a couple of my classes is all."

"Do you have any idea who took the photo?" I asked. I did not know what Tom was feeling but I wanted to slap this girl. Her total indifference was annoying to me.

"I wouldn't tell you if I did. I'm not a snitch," she said defiantly.

"Then you leave me only one option. Stand up and put your hands behind your back," I said rising.

Abby did what she was told, which surprised me. Tom read her the rights afforded to her by Miranda, as I handcuffed her behind her back, then turned to her parents. "She will be going with us to the police station. You may bring a lawyer down. If you cannot afford one, the court will appoint her one. She is being charged as an accessory to distribution of pornography involving a minor. It will be in her best interests to cooperate."

Mr. and Mrs. Stark stood stunned as we walked a handcuffed Abby from the room. We got her situated in the car and headed to the station.

In the back seat, Abby set up a diatribe. "You aren't really arresting me. I haven't done anything wrong. You guys just get off on pushing kids around. Wait until my parents get to the station. Dad will have your jobs. You made a big mistake this time."

Tom looked at me and smiled. Neither of us commented on what Abby had to say. Once we arrived at the station, Abby was turned over to the booking officer who took her fingerprints and mug shot. At some point, she shut up. I actually think she was frightened, especially when she was put in the holding cell with a couple of hookers.

It made my day to see this brat get a comeuppance. I began the paperwork from the interview with Matt Alexander and got forms ready for the interview to come with Abby Stark. It was going to be an interesting evening.

CHAPTER NINE

I was sitting at my desk when I heard the commotion at the door. Looking up I saw JJ coming though with boxes of pizza. Behind him came Sally Mae and Eli on his crutches. They were a sight for sore eyes. Tom was pointing them toward the break room with their bundles. My stomach rumbled as I got a whiff of the aroma coming from the boxes. I stood up from my desk and followed them into the break room. Sally Mae had a bag full of pop and salad. As always, she thought of everything. I took the bag Eli was carrying; it was filled with paper plates, napkins, paper cups, and plastic silverware. In no time, dinner was on the table and we were digging in.

"What made you guys decide to bring food?" Tom asked between bites of pizza.

There were some sidelong looks between JJ and Eli, before JJ answered, "This guy was getting antsy at the bunkhouse, and it was getting close to dinnertime. Seemed like a fun thing to do."

Eli grinned sheepishly, "Yeah, pretty much how it happened."

I smiled and continued to eat my salad. There were some really good cheese filled breadsticks, too.

Sally Mae finished getting everyone served and joined us. "Are you guys going to work all night on this case?"

"We have one more interview tonight. I'm hoping the girl decides to cooperate," I replied.

"It's a good thing. I was sure we were going to have to listen to Eli pace the bunkhouse all night long." She laughed.

"Hey, not true," Eli protested.

We all laughed. I think we knew Eli missed the job as much as he missed me.

When we finished up, Sally Mae and JJ put the empty boxes in the trash and we saved the leftovers for others on the staff. Things left in the break room had a way of disappearing. Tom and I got ready for our interview with Abby Stark. Eli found a chair and made himself comfortable.

Mr. and Mrs. Stark showed up with a lawyer in tow. The man was nattily dressed in a dark blue suit. He carried his briefcase and seemed to know his way around the station.

"Mom," Abby wailed from inside the holding cell.

"I would like a word with my client," the attorney said to the nearest officer.

The officer pointed toward Tom and me and said, "They are the arresting officers."

The attorney promptly headed our way looking like a bull in a china shop. "I want a room with some privacy and my client brought to me immediately," he said briskly.

Tom led him to an interrogation room, Mr. and Mrs. Stark followed meekly. Once inside, Mrs. Stark began crying. "Does she have to be in a cell?"

"She was put there until you arrived. I'll bring her in here now. Please impress upon her it's in her best interests to cooperate," Tom replied. He left the room to get Abby.

He unlocked the door to the holding cell and told Abby to put her hands behind her back. He handcuffed her and led her to the interrogation room where her parents and attorney were waiting for her. Once inside, he uncuffed her and said, "Let me know when you are ready to talk."

Eli and I watched the exchange and I wondered how long it would take for the Starks and their lawyer to convince Abby it would be in her best interest to tell us what we wanted to know. We did not have long to wait. The lawyer opened the door and waved to us indicating we should come in.

Tom and I wasted no time complying. Once inside, the lawyer introduced himself as Rex Stout. "I believe you have some questions for my client?" he asked.

"We do," I replied. "Earlier at her home, we were questioning Miss Stark about whether or not she knew who took a nude photo of one of her classmates. She refused to answer which is why she's here."

Mr. Stout turned to Abby, "I believe Miss Stark has seen the error of her thinking and is now willing to answer your questions for consideration."

"Her answers will determine how much consideration she gets." The firmness of my voice spoke volumes. I would not brook any nonsense from her.

"Let's begin," Stout said as he took a seat next to Abby.

"Abby," I began, "do you know who took the photo of Michelle?"

"I'm not sure, but I think it was Ellie Wexford. She's taken lots of photos for Chelsie," Abby whispered. "She even has photos of me and if this gets out so will they."

Mrs. Stark gasped. Her husband reached for her hand.

I continued, "Why does she have all these photos?"

"She uses them against people she doesn't like. Or like Michelle, girls who go after her boyfriend," Abby admitted.

"What did you do for her to have a photo of you?" I asked. "Do you know of other girls who have been subjected to a mass mailing of photos?"

Abby shook her head from side to side. "Most of the girls get transferred to different schools or are homeschooled. The only other time I saw her do something like this was last year. She made a website of photoshopped pictures of Alana Grey and gave the website to a bunch of people. Alana left school a couple days later. I don't know what happened to her. I was on the cheerleading squad and was taking too much attention from Chelsie. She had my photo taken in the shower and showed it to me. I dropped cheerleading and we've been friends ever since."

"What was Alana's crime?" I asked."

"She was dating Chelsie's boyfriend. He even gave her his class ring," Abby answered.

"One last question, did you help Chelsie send out the picture of Michelle?" I asked looking directly at her.

"I sent the photo texts," she admitted. "I didn't know it would get me in this much trouble."

"Seeing you have been honest with us, I think we can let you go home with your parents tonight. I suspect there may be some charges, but your willingness to help will be in your favor. I'm going to ask you to surrender your cell phone to the district attorney. You will be forbidden from making any cell phone calls for a while. I think you should also plan to stay off the Internet until you are told otherwise," were the solemn words I spoke softly.

"Oh, thank you, officer," Mrs. Stark sobbed. She reached for her daughter to give her a hug.

Abby had reverted back to her aloof self and shrugged her mother away saying, "Let's get out of here."

The men shook hands and the Stark family and their lawyer left the station. I had about an hour of paperwork to do then I could go home.

Tom looked at me as I sat at my desk. "Macy, the paperwork will wait until morning. Your notes will remind you of anything you've forgotten. Take Eli and go home."

"Are you heading out?" I asked glancing at Eli.

Tom laughed, "You bet. I have a family waiting for me. Even though Sally Mae probably called Shannon, I know there will be food waiting when I get home." He put the file in his inbox and started toward the door. He looked back and said, "What *are* you waiting for?"

I hastened to clear my desk then turned to help Eli. He had his crutches set and was ready to go. I was actually looking forward to a long evening at home. We all headed to the parking lot.

CHAPTER TEN

The ride home was in quiet companionship. Eli took my hand as I drove. I had never given any thought to what it would be like to take him to my home. Maybe I anticipated anxiety or excitement, this comfortable feeling was better.

My home was a ranch with an attached garage. Someone had decided to raise the bedrooms and set them apart from the rest of the house, so I had four steps up to the bedroom floor. The living room and kitchen/dining area were on the main level. I had never figured out the reason for the layout, but the house seemed to fit me. I had decorated in pastels, cream for the kitchen and dining area, peach for the living room, with each of the three bedrooms in a water color, aqua, blue, and, lavender.

Once inside, Eli collapsed on my sofa and I sat down beside him, "I'm so glad you came home early."

He reached over and pulled me into his arms. "I planned it because I knew how much I'd miss you." He continued to hold me tight.

"I missed you too," I said hugging him back. "I'm so glad I got to meet your family."

"They loved you," he whispered. "I knew they would."

"They were a bit overwhelming at first," I admitted. "I've never been around so many people who were all part of one family."

He looked me in the eyes and said, "Get used to it, Macy. I want you to be a part of my life for a long time."

Stunned I could only stare. We had only known each other for a couple of weeks and I was unsure of my feelings. How could I agree to a long-term commitment?

Eli must have sensed my misgivings. He leaned in and gave me a quick kiss, just enough to make me wish for more, then said, "Take all the time you need, I'm not going anywhere."

I snuggled into his arms and we sat there for a while, just the two of us, no sound but our breathing. When I realized Eli had fallen asleep, I quickly extricated myself and went upstairs. I made sure everything in the spare room was ready and turned down the bed. When I returned to the living room to help Eli, I found him awake and getting up.

"Let me help you," I said.

"I have to start walking without the crutches, I might as well start now," he said making his way slowly toward me.

I waited holding my breath and ready to move to him if he needed me. He did well getting to the steps.

"Sure glad there are only four steps," he chuckled reaching for the rail.

"I can help if you need it," I offered.

"Let me see how I do with the first step."

He slowly maneuvered the first step, then the second. I came up one step to be on hand. Eli proved very capable of navigating them all. He turned into the first room on the right.

"Wow the bed looks inviting," he said making his way toward it.

"I hope you'll be comfortable. The bathroom is across the hall and there's a nightlight to help guide you," I said feeling as though I were giving directions to a niece or nephew.

"I promise to be a good patient," he said sitting on the edge of the bed.

Slowly I walked to the bed, sat beside him, and said, "I'll try to be quiet in the morning. Are you going to be okay here all day by yourself?"

He took both my hands, "Macy, I've been on my own for a long time. I can manage a day by myself. Tom told me you have a workout room up here. I might try it out."

"Don't overdo it. I don't want to hear an emergency unit has been sent here." I chuckled. Eli took me in his arms again and gave me a thorough breath-stopping kiss. "Stop worrying and get some sleep. I'll be fine."

I stood and left the room. *That* kiss was going to have me thinking about it for a while. I was so glad he had come into my life. Surprisingly sleep came easily and quickly to me.

Tuesday

Not used to having company, I sensed someone in my room bringing me wide awake. My alarm had not gone off. I opened my eyes to find Eli sleeping in my rocking chair and wondered how long he had been there. Looking at my clock, I saw my alarm would not go off for another hour, but a cup of tea was sitting next to it. When I picked it up, I discovered it still warm, which made me think Eli was not really sleeping. I tossed my pillow at him.

He jumped when it hit him. "Hey!"

"How long have you been up?" I asked.

"About half an hour, I did fifteen minutes on your treadmill, and then made some coffee and your cup of tea. It was nice sitting here watching you sleep," he said sheepishly.

"Okay, next time wake me then I can do my work out while you're walking," I said as I grabbed my robe and pulled it on. I stood and headed for the bathroom my cup of tea in hand.

Eli rose slowly and headed for the guest bedroom. I came out with my sweats on ready for my morning workout. When I was done, I headed for the shower and could hear Eli in the kitchen. The smell of breakfast brought me to the kitchen sooner than later.

"You're a guest, meaning I should be cooking for you," I remarked as I walked into the kitchen. The smells from the stove were tantalizing. "What's to eat?" I worried my quick trip into the market on Sunday night had not yielded much.

"I rummaged around and found the makings for an omelet. Hope it's okay with you?" he asked casually dishing up our food.

I took a seat at the table and noted there was a pot of tea waiting for me. I filled my cup as I waited for Eli to join me. He had also made orange juice from the oranges I had and there was toast. Breakfast was a delightful change from my quick bowl of cereal and tea on the go. I could get used to this.

CHAPTER ELEVEN

Once at my desk, I finished the work I had put away last night. I was making a cup of tea when he walked into the break room.

"How's it going Macy?" he sounded chipper and was smiling.

"Things are wonderful. Where do you want to start today? Are we interviewing kids at school?" I asked picking up my cup.

Tom just looked at me, poured some coffee, and followed me into the office. "What do you suggest?"

I thought for a minute then answered, "I want to track down Alana Grey and I want to know more about Ellie Wexford. I think I'll call Mrs. Sweeny and enlist her help."

"It's worth a try. I sure don't want to wear out our welcome at the school," he commented dryly.

"Oh, we've already done it," I replied with a chuckle as I reached for the phone to dial the school. I was hoping Mrs. Sweeny would be able to help.

Mrs. Sweeny picked up the phone and identified herself. I told her who I was and asked about Alana Grey and Ellie Wexford. She asked for my fax number and said she would fax me the information she had. She also added Ellie was a sly one with her camera always around her neck. I thanked her and hung up.

In moments, the fax machine was spitting out information. I gathered it up wanting to look at Alana Grey first. Since she was being home schooled, it was my belief we would do best to start there.

I handed Tom the information and he read it. "You're right, Macy, we need to talk to Alana Grey first. Let's get the car and head there."

I grabbed the file we had been using for all the kids. We still had to talk to Katelyn Walker and I had a few more questions for Matt. This was nowhere near over.

In the car, I called ahead to speak with Mrs. Grey. Since this was a home school situation, they could be at a museum, art gallery, or another location.

"Hello," said the voice on the phone.

"May I speak with Helen Grey please?" I asked.

"This is she. May I ask who is calling?" She asked pleasantly.

"This is Detective Sergeant Macy McVannel with the Rivers Edge Police Department. My partner and I would like to talk to you and your daughter, Alana, about why she is no longer in school."

"How I choose to educate my daughter is not a police matter," she hissed venomously.

"Mrs. Grey, no one is questioning how your daughter is getting her education. A young girl at the high school is lying in a coma and we think your daughter might be able to help us," I responded quickly.

"We are at home today if you wish to come by," she said almost as if she were resigned to the idea.

"Thank you. We should be there in about fifteen minutes," I told her and hung up. I looked at Tom, "This is not going to be pleasant."

"None of them have been so far," he answered keeping his eyes on the road.

We were at the Grey home in close to fifteen minutes. Located in an older section of town, the home was surprisingly well-kept even though many others were run-down. Someone spent a great deal of time making this house look warm and welcoming. Flowers flourished in abundance and the old shade tree added to the home's appeal.

An attractive woman opened the door as we got out of the car. I could only assume she was Helen Grey as she was too old to be Alana. Her auburn hair was pulled up in a ponytail and she looked very comfortable in her jeans and t-shirt. She greeted us with a smile and invited us in.

She led us to a comfortable living room where Alana was already seated. We each took a seat and Mrs. Grey offered us a cup of tea or coffee. We declined and began our interview.

"I am Detective Sergeant Macy McVannel," I began. "This is my partner Detective Tom Maxwell," I gestured toward Tom. "We have some questions about what led to your decision to home school Alana."

Mrs. Grey sighed, "I wish you had been concerned when this all started."

"When what all started?" I asked wondering if it had been a police matter at the time.

Alana looked at her mom who nodded, took a deep breath, and said, "Last year, I started dating Matt Alexander. It was great for the first week. There was this girl, Chelsie, who started telling me to back off. She seemed to think Matt was her boyfriend even though he avoided her whenever he could. When Matt and I continued to have lunch together and date, it got worse. First, my books would get knocked out of my arms. Papers would end up missing. Then my lunch tray would get knocked to the floor. I'd have to clean it up before I could get a new one. Everyone would laugh. Matt and his friends usually helped, but it seemed to get worse when they did. Finally, after I had been to the counselor, a link to this website was sent to everyone. The site was called 'Sexy Kitten.' It had all these photos of some girl half dressed with my head on them. The site said I was the person in the photos and had some pretty provocative suggestions on it. When I showed it to my mom, she went to the school. They said nothing could be done and I should expect to get picked on if I continued to put up stuff like it. I couldn't go back." Tears rolled down her cheeks as she told us about her experience.

"Did you go to the police with this, Mrs. Grey?" I asked.

She shook her head no saying, "After the way the school reacted, I figured the police would not be able to do anything either. Should I have come to you?"

I nodded, "Yes, it constitutes distribution of pornography and our computer techs could have found out who was behind it. We could have stopped them."

"You said something about another girl having trouble?" she asked eagerly.

"Yes, Michelle Watson, also dated Matt Alexander, and Chelsie went after her. Chelsie's actions were enough for Michelle to attempt to take her life."

"Is she going to be okay?" Alana wanted to know.

"We don't know. She has not regained consciousness. It's the reason we are investigating all of this," I replied.

Alana wiped her tears, "How can I help? I know I was not the first girl something happened to. I don't want anyone else to get hurt."

"I appreciate your wanting to help. The prosecution may call you to testify. Are you willing?" I asked.

"Oh, yes. I can give you the website address. I don't know if it's still there, but maybe your people can check," she said eagerly.

"It would be great. I'll get them looking right away," I responded turning to Mrs. Grey. "I want to thank you for seeing us. I know this can't have been easy for either of you. Will Mr. Grey be home soon?"

"There is no Mr. Grey," she answered calmly. "He left us years ago. The only thing he does is pay his child support regularly."

"I'm glad he does," I said sincerely. I stood and Tom and I shook hands with both of them. We let ourselves out.

"WOW! CHELSIE HAS been in the porn business for a while," I said once we got into the car.

"Why don't you call the techs, have them go over her computer for the address Alana gave us?" Tom suggested.

I looked at his notes for the URL (Uniform Resource Locator) the first part of a web address, so I could call the techs and give it to them. I called as soon as I located it; gave the address to them, told them what we were looking for, and also had them check to see if it was still an active site.

"Should we call Matt Alexander and see if he can back up what Alana said?" Tom asked.

"We will, but I want to talk to him when his parents aren't around," I replied. "I think he will cooperate, he is not linked to any wrong doing. His father will protest our wanting to talk to him again." I contemplated the rest of my answer before saying, "Maybe we should have Sarah Stephens call him in. His dad could hire an attorney and come. We can feed Sarah the questions we need answered."

"Good idea. Let's run it by Sarah," Tom answered.

We drove to the ADA's office and stopped to see if Sarah had a minute or two for us. Her secretary told us she would be free in a minute if we could wait. We took seats to wait; it was just minutes when Sarah Stephens opened her door.

"Macy, Tom," she said politely, "come on it." She stood aside so we could enter her office. We took seats facing her desk; she closed the door, and sat at her desk. "Tell me how I can help."

"We have arrested Chelsie Patton a seventeen year old high school student for sending out the photo of Michelle Watson on the Internet. She was assisted by Abby Stark, who has cooperated and been released to her parents pending charges. While investigating we talked to Matt Alexander," I told her. "He is not involved in this, however this is not the first girlfriend he's had who has been attacked in some way, we need to ask him questions, but don't think his father will allow it."

"So you need me to invite the young man and his father in," Sarah stated.

Tom who had been silent answered, "Yes. We have to know what he knows about the website set up to make Alana Grey look like a porn queen."

"There is a second victim? Is she alive?" asked a horrified Sarah.

"She is alive and she is the only other victim we know of so far, but Matt indicated it has happened several times," I replied. "This is what we need to know, how many times and who the other girls are."

"I'd say we do," Sarah said angrily. "What makes you think the father will interfere?"

"He was adamant Matt not get involved," I responded. "I have the impression Matt would cooperate in any way he can. He's become a victim of Chelsie Patton, too."

"I'll have my secretary get Mr. Alexander on the phone and will impress upon him, he and his son need to report to this office within the hour," Sarah said. "He will be told he can bring his own attorney with him. Give me a list of your questions."

I had made a list of questions on the way over and handed the list to Sarah. She glanced at it and nodded. "My secretary will take notes so if other questions come up we will have them on record."

Tom and I stood. I extended my hand and said, "Thanks, Sarah, I knew we could count on you."

We left feeling much better about how part of the investigation would go. I personally was not looking forward to facing Mr. Alexander again. His better-than-everyone-else opinion of himself was annoying.

CHAPTER TWELVE

It was time for us to track down Ellie Wexford, photo bug extraordinaire. I made a call to Mrs. Sweeney who told me Ellie had not reported to school this morning. I wondered if she was looking for a place to hide. We had one of her friends in custody and had talked with a second.

"I see she lives with her dad. Should we call him first?" asked Tom.

"He would call and warn his daughter we're coming," I said thoughtfully. "According to this file she just turned eighteen, so we don't need a parent."

"We're just going to show up," he said. "We can get her for truancy then hit her with questions about her photography."

I liked his thinking. This would be a blitz attack. She would not have time to hide evidence or leave the house. I quickly made a call to Sarah Stephens. We needed to have techs and a search warrant en route.

The drive to the Wexford home took us a mile out of town; to a hunting cabin someone had attempted to turn into a bungalow. There was an older model Volkswagen Beetle in the driveway. The car had been painted in neon stripes. It was my guess Ellie was at home. We pulled in blocking any exit she might want to make. We approached the house on a path between flowerbeds overflowing with weeds. The house itself needed siding or a paint job. It had a vacant look rather than one of welcome. Tom rapped his knuckles on the door.

Ellie Wexford spiky, hot pink hair opened the door. She looked quickly beyond us as if expecting someone. Refocusing on us she said, "Yeah?"

"Ellie Wexford?" I asked knowing the answer already.

Giving me a once over she asked, "What if I am?"

"I'm Detective Sergeant Macy McVannel and this is my partner, Detective Tom Maxwell, we'd like to talk to you about missing school today," I said calmly.

"Truancy cops," she snorted.

"Something of the sort," I agreed. "May we come in?"

"Like, do I got to talk to you?" she wanted to know.

"Yes, I'm afraid you do," I replied.

She stood back allowing us to enter. The house showed serious neglect. Paper food containers sat on the end tables, pop bottles and beer cans were scattered on the floor. The beige carpet looked as if it had not been vacuumed in months. I heard music blaring in a room at the back of the house.

Ellie stood waiting for us to say something. When we did not she quipped, "Sorry, it's the maid's day off."

Tom was unimpressed. "Tell us why you chose not to go to school today."

"Forgot to set my alarm, decided I could miss a day. No big deal," she answered shrugging.

"Isn't your father supposed to call in for you?" I asked.

"Nah, I'm eighteen. I can call in for myself, thought it was a waste of time." She had an answer for everything. I guessed this was not new.

"Your car in the driveway?" Tom asked.

"The bug, yeah," she answered beaming.

"I'm guessing you did the paint job," Tom kept at it.

"Sure did. I love messing with paint."

This piqued my interest. "Is paint the only medium you work in?"

"No, I do photography, too. Mostly black and white wanna see my set up?" she asked.

We were not going to get a better offer. Tom responded quickly, "Great. I've always wanted to learn photography."

Following Ellie, we went through the disgusting kitchen, out a back door to a well-worn path leading to a small shed. I was surprised at how neat and clean the shed was. Chemical bottles were lined neatly on shelves and labeled. The work counter was spotless. The contrast to the house was startling.

Ellie walked toward a table and pulled out her latest collection of photos. She had been shooting the football team at practice. The pictures were stunning. She had zeroed in on each player and captured his essence. She was good at what she did. Tom admired her photos.

"How do you decide what lighting you need?" he asked.

"Depends on where I am. These were taken outside and natural light is best," she replied warming to the subject. "Look at these." She pulled a different file out. "These were over exposed, but I like them."

The photos were taken in a park, people picnicking, playing Frisbee, or softball, and children running. Even over exposed, they were beautiful. The girl had talent.

"Would you look at a photo I have and tell me about it?" Tom asked innocently.

"Sure, no problem," she reached for the photo he had pulled from his jacket.

Her hand shook as she recognized the photo. She looked between Tom and I a deer caught in the headlights expression on her face. It took only a moment for her snarky personality to return.

"Isn't this some kind of entrapment?" She wanted to know.

"Entrapment is when we get you to do something illegal. We just showed you a photo," I replied.

"Yeah, well I don't like it," she whined as she shoved the photo back at Tom.

"Maybe you should tell us why you took it," he said taking the photo.

"Ha, I didn't take *that* trash," her reply was vehement.

"We have a witness who says you did," I responded. "We also have a search warrant for everything on the premises coming any minute. Do you really want our techs tearing apart your little studio here?"

"Wait, just wait," she said obviously stalling. She put her hand on her forehead as if thinking what to do next. "Okay, what do you want to know?"

"For starters where are the photos you took for Chelsie Patton? Including all negatives," I said bluntly.

She turned and pulled a file out from behind a row of bottles. Reluctantly she put it in Tom's outstretched hand. "Is it all?" she asked sounding put out by the whole thing.

"It's only the beginning," I answered. "We need to know why you took the photos."

"Simple, she pays good money," was the flip answer.

"You don't care she uses these photos to ruin others?" I was incredulous.

"She just pays me to take photos. I don't know what she does with them," Ellie shrugged. "I'm not her inner circle. Those girls are too snooty for me."

"Did you know she sent this photo out on the Internet?" Tom asked.

"I heard about it after the fact, doesn't make it my fault," she snipped.

"It makes you her accomplice," I told her. "It means in the eyes of the law you are part of her crime."

"No way! I didn't do anything but take pictures," she protested.

"Pictures in the locker room and who knows where else," Tom said disgustedly. "Did you help her set up the website which was supposed to be Alana Grey?"

"No, I don't mess with the Internet, it has no soul," she stated. "She got some guy to do it for her, but I don't know him."

A squad car and the crime van arrived, Ellie seeing it out the window screeched, "You said they didn't have to come through here and mess things up!"

"We didn't make you any promises," I countered. "At the moment you are under arrest as accessory to distribution of pornography." I pulled out my handcuffs and Ellie looked wildly at me. Then I continued, "Ellie Wexford, you have the right to remain silent anything you say can and will be used against you in a court of law. You have the right to an attorney, if you cannot afford one, one will be appointed for you."

I slipped the cuffs on her wrists, as she stood there speechless. We walked her to the squad car, told them to take her to the station, book her as an accessory to distribution of pornography, and let her call her father. The officer led her to the car, helped her into the back, and drove away.

The techs wanted to know what we were looking for; we told them anything looking like pornography. They went to work looking for hidden files. Silently we walked to the car.

"She wasn't what I expected," I told Tom.

"I understand. All that talent and no good outlet," he replied frowning. "I wonder where her father is. You think now might be the time to call him?"

"No, but now might be the time to find out something about him. Something about this situation does not sit right with me," I said then put in a call to have a records check done on Chase Wexford and was assured it would be on my desk when I arrived back at the office.

CHAPTER THIRTEEN

When we returned to the station, Tom headed to the break room. I could see he needed some space so I let him go. This case had been eating at him from a parent's perspective. His kids would eventually attend Rivers Edge High School. This case was really coming at him where it hurt.

I called Eli to see how his day was going.

"Well, your neighbors have been over and checked me out. I think I passed inspection," he chuckled.

"Oh, no, my reputation is gone," I replied laughing.

"No, I told them my intentions, so I don't think you have anything to worry about," he retorted.

"Your *intentions*. Are they something I should know about?" I asked in all seriousness.

"Only if you want to," he said and I could hear the smile in his voice. It made me think of our goodnight kiss.

"I think we should discuss this after dinner," I told him as I felt the heat of a blush creep up my cheeks.

"Sounds good, and I hope you haven't made any plans. Sally Mae and JJ are coming dinner at seven," he said.

"Seven is good, I'll see you then," I answered ringing off.

"Seven is good for what?" Tom asked.

"Dinner with Sally Mae and JJ," I answered reaching for a file in my inbox. "Just got the file on Chase Wexford, he's a long haul trucker. Makes me wonder what the mother was thinking to give him custody," I said speaking my thoughts aloud.

"Wonder where the mother is?" Tom mused then went on, "The call I got was from the techs at the Wexford house. They found a hidden safe but could not get it open. They are bringing it in. Maybe we can work a deal if Ellie tells them how to open it. There were a ton of photos of different students, mostly girls. They are bringing those, too." He took a breath before continuing, "We are going to need to look at them before we talk to her or Chelsie again. This is bigger than we thought."

Ellie was a puzzle to me. She was not the type of girl Chelsie Patton ran around with. There was no family money; she was not what Chelsie would consider upper crust elite. What brought the two of them together? Ellie was a wonderful photographer and could have a great future ahead of her. This mess was going to put a damper on it.

I opened it to see the information on Chase Wexford. "Uh oh."

Tom hung up his phone. "Interesting," he commented.

"I'll listen, but we have a problem," I said handing him the file and reaching for the phone.

"What?" Tom asked. Tom looked at what I had read and stared at me. "You think we ought to get her out now?" he asked.

"No, I think this is the safest place for her," I responded.

Chase Wexford had a criminal history in the porn industry. It seems he featured his young daughter in a couple of his early films.

"How did he get custody of her?" Tom asked. "I mean what judge in his right mind would put an abused minor child with her abuser?"

"ADA Stephens, office. How may I help you?" Came the professional voice of her secretary.

"This is Macy McVannel. I need to talk to Ms. Stephens as soon as possible about a case we are working on," I responded.

"Hold one minute, please," the voice answered and pushed the hold button.

I looked at Tom and said, "Elevator music," while rolling my eyes.

"She won't be long," he said.

I put up one finger as Sarah spoke into the phone, "This is Sarah Stephens."

"Macy here. We have a serious problem with one of the witnesses in this case," I told her.

"What kind of problem?" Stephens asked.

"Seems she's been in the custody of her father for a good many years and he's used her in some of his own porn movies," I said.

"Oh, good grief. How long has he had her? How many times has he used her in films? Is this going to impact what we already have? Get Tom and get here *now*," she finished not even waiting for me to answer. She hung up the phone.

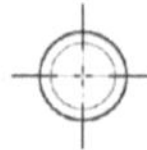

I STOOD GRABBING the file on Chase Wexford and headed for the door with Tom right beside me. When we got to the car, we both started talking at once then laughed.

"You go first," he said laughing.

"Why on earth would her mother let the girl go back to the man who abused her?" I asked with disbelief.

"I don't know," he answered. "Do you want a quick rundown on what the techs found?"

"Yeah, give me something else to focus on," I replied.

"It seems the techs found more photos of young girls in various stages of nudity," he said in a rush. "They followed orders and did not wreck the place."

"She has a ton of talent and a prison sentence is going to ruin any chances she has to make a go of it."

We arrived at the courthouse, parked, and made our way to the ADA's office.

HER SECRETARY LOOKED up when we entered and said, "Go right in, she's expecting you."

We entered Sarah's office, closing the door behind us. She had been looking out the window and turned when we entered.

"Is this going to blow us out of the water?" she asked.

Tom took the initiative, "I don't think so. At this moment, all we have on this girl is she took some photos. She was paid for taking them."

Sarah looked at me as if waiting for me to disagree. When I did not she said, "I have talked to Matt Alexander. His father and an attorney came blustering in here like they were in charge. It only took a minute for the attorney to see Matt was just a witness and shut the father up. I had a court recorder in here and took his statement as a deposition. It's been transcribed for you. My secretary will have copies for you on your way out. Now, tell me about this girl."

"Her name is Ellie Wexford. She just turned eighteen and has lived with her father for the past ten years. We are still tracking down the mother and how she ended up with her father," I told her.

"Apparently when she was three or four dad was caught taking nude photos of himself with her. He claims they were innocent photos, but they ended up on the Internet in some porn sites. He was selling them to make extra money," Tom added.

"So, this girl who takes pornographic photos has been exposed to this all her life. What is her actual crime?" Sarah asked.

"As far as we can tell, taking photos of unsuspecting people in places where photos should not be taken. The school locker room," I said. "I don't believe she intended them to go out on the Internet."

"So intent to distribute is not a charge?" Sarah confirmed.

"Not at this time," I agreed.

"Okay, do your research on the mother, hold the girl as long as you can and find out if the father has any involvement in all of this," Stephens said dismissing us.

We rose said our good-byes and picked up our copies of what Matt Alexander had told her.

"MACY," TOM SAID as we got back to the office, "I'm calling it a day. I can't deal with this. I need to be with my kids."

"Go, I'll get the search going on Ellie's mom, read through Matt's statement and head on home," I told him.

He smiled wanly and left the squad room. I sat at my desk and typed in the search parameters to begin looking for Ellie Wexford's mother. Then I started reading Matt's statement.

Those present: Sarah Stephens ADA, Matthew Alexander, Bradley Alexander, Walter Windset, attorney for the Alexanders, and Marge Landon, court stenographer

Date: October 15

Location: office of the ADA

S. Stephens: Matthew, I understand you have been the target of some viciousness caused by one Chelsie Patton. Is this correct?

M. Alexander: Yes, Chelsie harasses my girlfriends.

S. Stephens: I understand Alana Grey left school because of the harassment and Michelle Watson is currently in the hospital. Is this correct?

M. Alexander: Yes, as far as I know.

S. Stephens: The detectives who came to talk to you seem to think there are other girls who have been affected. Are there other girls?

M. Alexander: Two, Mary Golden and Tansy Taylor, but I think Mary moved because her dad got a transfer.

S. Stephens: Can you tell me about the harassment?

M. Alexander: It starts out with one of Chelsie's friends telling the girl I am off limits. Then it proceeds to knocking her books to the floor, grabbing papers and tossing them, dumping lunch trays. I don't know what finally happened with Tansy, but the worst was the stupid website Chelsie had put up about Alana and now this photo of Michelle.

S. Stephens: You knew about the website with Alana?

M. Alexander: Some of the guys were laughing about it. I reported it to the computer teacher, Mr. Blackstone, and Mr. O'Brian, the principal.

S. Stephens: To your knowledge what was done about it?

M. Alexander: Mr. Blackstone, the computer teacher had it blocked somehow on the school computers. The next thing I knew Alana was gone. Mr. Blackstone left at the end of last year. I thought he got a job somewhere else.

S. Stephens: We'll look into it. Have you personally been harassed?

M. Alexander: Only if you count Chelsie hanging out at my locker and trying to hang on me. I usually just blow her off and tell her to get lost.

S. Stephens: Does she call or text you?

M. Alexander: I didn't give her my cell number. I don't give it to many people. So, she can't text or call. If she called me at home, I don't know. I don't take her calls.

S. Stephens: Does she message you on the computer?

M. Alexander: She is blocked from my Facebook page and I never gave her my e-mail address. As far as I know she has never messaged me.

S. Stephens: Did you at one time date Chelsie Patton?

M. Alexander: I danced with her a couple times at a dance when we were in the eighth grade. I thought she was cute. But she's boring. All she talks about is herself and being a Patton. She thinks she's above the rest of the world.

S. Stephens: Does Chelsie date anyone?

M. Alexander: I don't think so. She always has some guy on her arm for dances, but she never spends much time with them. Some I recognize, some I've never seen. None of my friends want anything to do with her.

S. Stephens: Thank you for your time. I appreciate you coming forward. I may have other questions as the case develops, may I call you?

M. Alexander: Yes, please call me anytime. Do you know if Michelle can have visitors?

S. Stephens: I'm sorry I don't know. How did you happen to meet Michelle?

M. Alexander: I was having some trouble with geometry and my teacher told me Michelle was tutoring after school as part of her National Honor Society requirements. I signed up. She has been a big help. She's also funny, interesting, and caring. Did you know she helps out at the soup kitchen?

S. Stephens: I did not know. It is nice to hear about our youth being involved. Again let me thank you for your time, gentlemen.

I looked at the clock when I was done reading. It had taken me less than an hour and there were three new victims for us to interview. Those interviews could wait until tomorrow. I was going home to Eli.

I put Matt's statement in the file, put the file in my basket for tomorrow, grabbed my purse, and left.

CHAPTER FOURTEEN

Tantalizing smells assaulted my nose when I entered the kitchen. Eli looked up from the stove smiling.

"Welcome home," he said. "JJ and Sally Mae should be here any minute."

"Smells wonderful in here, what are we having?" I asked as my stomach rumbled.

"I hope you like Italian. I made some lasagna and garlic bread. We have spinach salad, wine, oh yes, and a wonderful dessert sent over by your neighbors," he replied impishly.

"We need to talk about my neighbors," I said dryly.

Just then the doorbell rang; I went to let JJ and Sally Mae in. I got hugs from both and led them to the kitchen.

"Get settled at the table. I have the water almost ready for your tea. Hi, guys find a place," Eli said as he continued to get the dinner ready.

I sat at the table and Eli brought me a cup of tea, coffee for our guests, and a bowl of salad. "I made a special dressing for the salad, I hope you like it."

"Why didn't I know you could cook?" I asked sampling the salad.

"I try to keep it a secret until I know someone," he answered. "I went to culinary school before I became a police officer."

I looked up in surprise. "What made you change?"

"My dad died in the line of duty. My brothers all had careers. It was left to me to follow in his footsteps," he said quietly.

"I'm sorry," I replied not knowing what else to say.

"I'm not. I got to meet you." I looked at him to see him grinning from ear to ear.

"I hope it's not the only reason," I said looking at him.

"No, I get to cook when I am off duty. Which until lately hasn't been often," he said seriously. "Now everyone knows my secret, I'll be cooking lots of meals." His grin said he would enjoy cooking.

JJ chimed in, "So, I can get some cooking lessons?"

"Sure," Eli replied, "I enjoy showing off for others.

Sally Mae looked at me and rolled her eyes then said, "Boys.

"I guess I will soak this up while I can. Especially since my cooking leaves a lot to be desired," I told him with a chuckle.

He joined us at the table. When the salads were finished, he took the bowls and brought us the lasagna and garlic bread. He also filled our glasses with a red wine he had procured from somewhere. Everything was delicious. I knew I would be in need of my morning workouts even more if this kept up.

We finished with dessert in the living room. It was a raspberry crisp with cream cheese. Then Eli and JJ retreated to the kitchen to clean up. Eli explaining, "If you make the mess, it's your job to clean it up. The first rule of cooking is clean up."

Sally Mae gave me one of her knowing looks. "Anything happening with you two," she asked curiously.

"We are getting to know each other. I'm working a case and Eli is here healing," I replied ambiguously.

"Sure, you keep telling yourself it's the only thing going on," she kidded. "I am enjoying the new job. I like having Mike's mom to take care of and getting to know JJ's mom."

"How are they?" I asked earnestly glad to take the conversation off me.

"They are fine and becoming fast friends. I think it's Ida's doing," Sally Mae told me. "They do quilting three mornings a week. Each one takes a turn being the hostess."

I smiled. *It warmed my heart how to see all the good which had come out of solving Bobby James Appleton's murder.* "Sounds like fun. Someday maybe we will be like them," I said wistfully.

Sally Mae laughed, "Well we are going to have to learn to quilt, or something before it can happen."

I laughed seeing her point. The guys came in with coffee and tea. As we settled in to talk, it felt right old friends getting together and having conversation.

AFTER SALLY MAE and JJ left, I sat on the sofa, leaned back into Eli's waiting arms, and asked, "So what are these intentions you told my neighbors about?"

"I was honest with them and told them how much I admire you. My plans are to spend a long time getting to know you," he answered.

Finding myself somewhat disappointed with his answer I asked, "That's it?"

Eli laughed, pulled me toward him, and kissed me with the kind of soul shattering passion of dreams. When he finally stopped he asked, "Wasn't it enough?"

"Um," I said blushing before I kissed him again. Part of my brain was telling me to let go of the past and part was warning me to tread slowly. I ignored both.

We settled in to watch an old movie with the lights turned low. For the first time in years, I found myself completely relaxed and content.

I must have fallen asleep. I stretched, listening, and wondering what had woken me. Silence. I shoved off the blanket Eli had covered me with and slowly sat up. I sensed something amiss but could not put my finger on it.

"Lay down," a voice hissed.

I quickly lay back down whispering, "Eli?"

"Yes, someone is in the backyard. I don't want to give them a target if they are armed," he whispered.

"Why? What?" My brain was not functioning. *We were not in the bunkhouse hiding, this was my home.* "Where are you?"

"Behind the sofa with your weapon," he answered.

"What on earth?" I rolled to the floor. *I'm fully capable of defending myself. What is going on?* I looked toward the sliding door in the dining room; sure enough someone was creeping up to my back door. "Crawl to your right, I'm going to the left we should be able to take him when he comes through the door," I ordered and began moving. I heard Eli to my right making his way in the dark to the door. All the time I kept sight of the door. As soon as I was out of sight to anyone coming in, I stood next to the door ready to attack the person intent on coming through. Just as the glass broke, Eli rose on the other side.

In just seconds a hand came through the glass and unlocked the door, it slid slowly open and the person stepped in. We let him get fully inside before Eli yelled, "Freeze, put your hands in the air."

I slipped behind the person as he turned to run. The shock of seeing me stopped him and his hands rose slowly in the air. "On the floor place your hands behind your head," I said calmly.

"You guys have been watching too much TV," he quipped.

I flipped the switch and watched his face register shock as he saw the gun Eli had trained on him, "Do as the Detective tells you, son."

The young man quickly got down on the floor and placed his hands behind his back. I got my cuffs and put them on him. Then Eli helped me get him up and we sat him in a chair at my table.

"Do you want to tell us why you were breaking in here?" Eli asked.

He looked first at Eli then at me and hung his head. "The place was supposed to be empty."

"What made you think so?" I asked.

"I was told the lady cop who lived here had moved in with her boyfriend," he said sadly.

"Obviously someone gave you bad information," Eli stated. "You want to tell us now why you were breaking in?"

"I was hired to get some information," he said dully

"Who hired you?" I asked.

"What information?" Eli wanted to know.

"I'm not sayin' any more. I want a lawyer," was the sullen reply.

I moved to the phone and called dispatch. I told them we had captured a youthful home invader and needed transport for him. They responded transport was five minutes away.

I moved back to the table. "Looks like we'll need to go in and make report," I told Eli. Transport in about five minutes."

"Can you handle him?" Eli asked.

"No problem." I took my gun from Eli and returned it to its holster. We waited in silence for the transport officers to arrive. I met them at the front door.

One patrolman took photos of the broken door while the other read the young man his rights. As he led the boy to the car, the other asked me for a statement. I told him we would be following them in to give a full report. He nodded and left the house. We locked up as best we could. Eli found some plywood in the garage and we put it against the door, then moved the table over to hold it up.

We headed out to my car.

"I wonder what he was looking for and who told him the house was empty?" I said thoughtfully.

"Maybe being booked and a talk with his lawyer will get us the information," Eli suggested.

"So much for a relaxing evening at home," I muttered.

Eli chuckled but reached for my hand.

CHAPTER FIFTEEN

It took less than ten minutes to reach the station. Eli and I went in and found the arresting officers. The young man, identified as Dustin Bell a nineteen year old who had attended Rivers Edge High School, was in a holding cell. His parents were notified and coming in with an attorney.

"Do you think Eli and I can sit in on the questioning?" I asked. "His break in attempt might be connected to a case we're working on."

"You can watch through the two-way," Officer Page replied. He had introduced himself and his partner Officer Boyle when we reached the station to give our statements.

Mr. and Mrs. Bell arrived with an attorney who looked like he had just rolled out of bed, rumpled suit and wild hair. They were shown into an interview room and Dustin was taken in to talk with them. Page said, "His attorney is Mad Miller."

"Mad Miller?" I asked surprised to see the legend.

"Yeah, Mad Bart Miller, available twenty-four hours a day for the down trodden," Page answered sarcastically. "Does some crazy things trying to get his clients off."

I looked at Eli and shook my head. Mad Miller had a reputation for the outrageous. I had never met him before.

A few minutes later Miller opened the door and indicated they were ready to begin.

Eli and I went to the room where we would be able to see and hear what was going on. Page and Boyle entered the interrogation room.

Page started, "Dustin you are being charged with breaking and entering. We'd like to know why you were breaking into the home of a police officer."

Mad Miller answered, "What's in it for my client if he talks?"

"My word he cooperated, when this comes before the judge," Page answered.

"I'm not sure it's enough," Miller said slowly.

"I am not here to make deals. Deals are something you have to take up with the ADA. I need to know what Dustin was doing and why," Page said with authority.

"You may speak now, Dustin," Miller said.

"I was paid to get the detective's laptop," he answered.

"Who paid you?" Page asked.

"Chelsie Patton," Dustin said hanging his head. Then he mumbled, "I'm a dead man."

"What do you mean you're a dead man?" Page and Miller asked simultaneously.

Dustin whipped his head up and said, "She told me she'd kill me if I told."

"Are you aware Chelsie is in police custody at this time?" Page asked.

"Uh no," he answered.

"You didn't know she was arrested at school yesterday?" Page asked in disbelief.

"I graduated and was home with the flu," he answered and his mother nodded in agreement.

"How did she get in contact with you?" Page asked.

"Katelyn Walker sent me a text with all the information. She is the one who always contacts me when Chelsie has a job for me," Dustin replied.

"How do you get paid?" Page asked.

"Um I don't know if I should say," Dustin said.

"It's okay to tell them," Miller coaxed.

"Katelyn and I have sex and she leaves me an envelope of money when we're done," he said quietly.

Mrs. Bell gasped.

"So, you prostitute yourself for her?" Page asked.

"Um no. I get to have sex with a cute girl," he replied. "She wouldn't look at me if Chelsie didn't tell her to."

"I see. Have you done this before?" Page asked.

"Sure, I do computer stuff for Chelsie all the time," Dustin said proudly.

"How many times has this happened?" Page asked.

Dustin thought for a minute before answering, "Probably I've done things for Chelsie four times in the past. Katelyn and I hook up about once a month for the past couple years."

"What did Chelsie think would be on the detective's laptop?" Page asked.

"I'm not sure, she just wanted it wiped clean," Dustin answered.

Page looked at Miller, "I think we can get him a deal, but he'll have to testify against Chelsie and replace the window he broke tonight."

Miller nodded apparently satisfied with the way things had gone.

I had been taking notes. I now had more information against Chelsie and I wanted to talk to Katelyn Walker first thing in the morning. Eli and I waited until the officers left the interrogation room.

"Officer Page, thank you for allowing us to listen. You have helped my case against Chelsie Patton," I said.

"Anytime, will the kid get off easy?" he asked.

"Probably probation until he's twenty-one, but I suspect his sex life will be curtailed," I answered with a smile.

Eli and I shook hands with Page and Boyle and headed to my car. Once inside I drove us home.

Inside the house, Eli was trying to figure out a way to prevent any more unwanted visitors.

"Eli, leave the table against it for now. I'll call the insurance company in the morning and get someone out here to replace it. Come to bed," I told him.

Eli turned grinning, "Is *that* an invitation?"

I blushed realizing what I had said. Then I turned and went upstairs without answering. I changed into my pajamas and crawled into my bed thinking, *'McVannel, you are an idiot.'*

A few minutes later, Eli sat on the edge of my bed, "Macy, I'm sorry. I was kidding."

"I know," I mumbled.

"Maybe I should think about moving back to my apartment," he said.

I did not respond.

He leaned across me and his lips found mine. I felt as though I was losing myself in the passion. "I love you," he whispered against my lips. Then he left the room.

I rolled over letting tears fall against my pillow thinking, *I have to move on. I'm so afraid. I'm starting to love you, too, Eli.*

CHAPTER SIXTEEN

Wednesday

I awoke with a sense something was wrong. Quickly I grabbed my robe putting it on as I peeked in on Eli. He was not in his bed; it had not been slept in. *Did he leave?* I hoped not. Tip-toeing down the stairs I saw JJ sleeping in a chair. Eli was asleep on the sofa. On the coffee table sat an empty wine bottle and several beer bottles. I just shook my head and went back upstairs.

I changed into my sweats for my workout and let the guys sleep. I had not heard JJ come in so they must have been very quiet. I finished up, took my shower, and dressed for work. Entering the kitchen, I found both men busy cleaning up from last night and making breakfast.

"Good morning, JJ what brings you here so early?" I asked.

"Macy, you know I was here all night," he answered, "I saw you sneaking around this morning. I came to help Eli guard the place."

I laughed knowing I had been caught, "Guard the place?"

Eli piped in as he handed me a cup of tea, "I was worried someone else might try breaking in." He nodded his head toward the makeshift blockade.

"I'll call the insurance company on my way to work," I assured him.

"Good, JJ and I plan to have it replaced today," Eli said.

"I can hire someone to do it," I protested.

"It's handled, Macy," Eli said with authority.

I smiled remembering his whispered words. We settled in as best we could at the table and had breakfast together. Then I went to work.

The first thing on the agenda today was an interview with Katelyn Walker. I was sure Tom would be in the break room. I was wrong. He was sitting at his desk reading the transcript of Matt Alexander.

"Hey, Macy, heard you had some trouble last night."

"Nothing we couldn't handle, but the intruder is directly related to our case," I told him.

"How?"

"He was hired by none other than Chelsie Patton. She's been trading the sexual services of one Katelyn Walker to get this guy to do her hacking," I told him disgustedly.

"I suppose Katelyn Walker will be in school?"

"My guess, too. I sure don't want to interview her there," I replied.

"Let's call her parents and get them to bring her in," Tom suggested.

"I think it would be better if we got Sarah Stephens to call them in. I'm sure we could be there for the interview," I said.

"However you want to handle it," Tom shrugged as he said it.

I wondered what was going on with him. For the past two days he had been edgy and touchy about this whole case. Now it was as if he no longer cared. I went to get a cup of tea as I mulled this new attitude over.

Coming back to our desks I asked, "Tom, what's up with you? The past two days this case has had you uptight and angry. Today it's like you no longer care."

Tom leaned back in his chair, "I hate everything about this case. Last night Shannon and I had a long talk about it, from a parent's perspective. We have taught our boys right from wrong. We will teach Mimi the same way we taught the boys. I can only protect them so much. I need to separate my personal feelings from my professional feelings or I'm going to screw something up."

I was awed by this. Tom rarely let me into his feelings. We had been partners for six years and this was the first he had really opened up. I was glad he felt he could.

"I told you things would work out," I said. "Let's get started. Call Sarah and see what she thinks about interviewing Katelyn."

Tom said grabbed the phone. I could only hear Tom's side of the conversation, but it sounded as though it was going well.

Tom hung up the phone smiling and said, "Let's roll."

I grabbed the file with my notes and the information on the case and followed in his wake. We walked the two blocks to the courthouse and Sarah's office.

"Go right in," Marge told us when we arrived. "She's expecting you."

Tom knocked on the closed door; we entered and took the seats across from Sarah at her desk.

"So, what brings you in exactly?" Sarah asked quietly.

"We need to interview Katelyn Walker. She's most likely at school and we've worn out our welcome there," I answered.

"How does this young girl fit into all of this?" Sarah questioned.

I said, "There was a break-in at my home last night. When the young man was questioned by the arresting officers he said he'd been hired by Chelsie Patton through Katelyn Walker. Evidently as well as bringing money from Chelsie, she provides sexual entertainment for the young man."

"I can add pimping to the escapades of Chelsie Patton?" Sarah wanted to know.

"I don't know yet," was my reply.

"Do you have the information on this girl?" Sarah asked.

I opened the file and pulled out the sheet I had been given by Mrs. Sweeny at the school. I handed it to Sarah.

She took it and looked it over. "I need to think about how to handle this. We invited Matthew Alexander in with his father and attorney because he's a victim. This girl could well be a co-conspirator. We have to be careful so nothing is tainted." She thought for a moment then continued, "I'm going to see if I can get an arrest warrant for her based on the information you received last night. Wait here." She rose and walked to the outer office.

It took her a few minutes then she returned saying, "We should be able to catch Judge Allen before she starts her morning session."

We followed Sarah to the elevators and down to Judge Allen's chambers. Once in the judge's chambers, Sarah made her case for an arrest warrant. Judge Allen looked as us and asked, "Is this about the despicable young woman who was in my court on Monday?"

"Yes, your honor," I answered.

She nodded and signed the document. As she handed it back she said, "Please get this nonsense wrapped up quickly."

"Yes, Ma'am," Tom and I answered simultaneously.

The three of us left, leaving Sarah at the elevator. "I'll be at the station when you get there. Don't ask her anything but her name, read her Miranda, and cuff her. Let the school call her parents."

I nodded as Tom and I left for our car. Neither of us was looking forward to an encounter with Mr. O'Brian again, but this was the best way for this to go down.

Tom surveyed the lot as we got out of the car.

"What are you looking for?" I asked curiously.

"Stragglers," Tom answered nodding toward two boys high-tailing it to a side door.

I chuckled, "It's the presence thing again, right?"

"Sure is," Tom answered smiling.

We walked up the front steps and into the office. Mrs. Sweeny greeted us, "Detectives, how can we help you today?"

"Will you page Katelyn Walker to the office?" I asked.

"Certainly, do you need to use Mr. O'Brian's office again?" She asked walking to her desk.

"No, we're here to make an arrest," Tom answered quietly.

Mr. O'Brian entered from his office in time to hear Tom's comment. "What do you mean, you're here to make an arrest," he bellowed.

"Lower your voice, Mr. O'Brian, we want as little disruption as possible," I told him.

"You can't just walk in here and arrest students willy-nilly," he blustered.

"You're right," I said waving the arrest warrant in his face. "We have a warrant now return to your office or I'll arrest you for obstruction."

Mr. O'Brian blustered but backed toward his office. Mrs. Sweeny smiled and spoke in to her phone. "Please ask Katelyn Walker to come to the office. She's being signed out." She turned to me, "Can you sign her out?"

I signed on the line and wrote released into police custody. "Please wait until we leave then call her parents."

Mrs. Sweeny nodded and retreated to her desk. Tom and I waited for Katelyn to arrive.

It took just a few minutes for her to arrive carrying a jacket and her backpack. She nodded to us and asked, "Where are my parents?"

"You are under arrest. Your parents will join you at the police station," Tom told her. "Please put down your backpack and jacket."

She complied looking from one of us to the other.

"Please place your hands behind your back and listen to Detective Maxwell as he reads you your rights," I said taking out my handcuffs. As I cuffed her, Tom read her the rights afforded her under Miranda. When he asked if she understood, she just nodded in affirmation. I picked up her jacket and backpack, thanked Mrs. Sweeny, and led her to our car. Katelyn remained silent on the trip to the station.

When we arrived the booking sergeant took her for fingerprints and mug shots. She was read the charges of conspiracy to transmit pornography, and prostitution. She almost fainted at the last one.

Tom and I went to our desks. I called Sarah Stephens and told her we were back with Katelyn Walker. She said she would be at the station in about fifteen minutes. Tom and I knew her parents would arrive soon with an attorney in tow. I wondered how this interview would go. Tom wandered off for coffee.

CHAPTER SEVENTEEN

Sarah Stephens was heading toward my desk when the sound of a ruckus hit our ears.

"I demand to see my daughter," was the voice of an irate father.

"Who might your daughter be?" asked the desk officer calmly.

"My daughter is Katelyn Walker and two of your officers removed her from school without my permission," Mr. Walker bellowed.

Tom, Sarah, and I headed toward the commotion. Mr. Walker had an attorney tugging at him as he leaned over the counter toward the officer there.

"Mr. Walker," Sarah spoke calmly.

He turned to look at Sarah scowled and asked, "Who the hell are you?

"I'm Assistant District Attorney Sarah Stephens. I authorized the arrest of your daughter. If you'd come this way please," she responded and turned to walk toward the interrogation room.

Walker blustered for a few seconds however he and his attorney followed Sarah. Tom and I went to the adjoining room to hear what Sarah had to say.

"Be seated gentlemen," she said calmly. The men took seats across from her. "Katelyn was arrested for conspiracy to transmit pornography and prostitution. She'll be brought to you shortly. I would advise you to get her to cooperate if she wants any leniency from me." She turned and left the room.

Tom and I joined her in the hallway. "You can have the girl taken in now. I'm sure her father will have questions for her before she speaks to us. I'm guessing at least fifteen minutes before they come up with a plan."

"I'll get her." Tom said and walked toward the holding cells. He returned a few minutes later with a handcuffed Katelyn Walker. He led her into the interrogation room.

Mr. Walker could be heard through the door, "How dare you treat my daughter like a common criminal."

Tom looked at the man as he opened the door and replied, "She is a common criminal." He shut the door before Walker could start in again.

I shook my head. Sarah looked at her watch.

Tom looked at both of us and asked, "What's with the watch?"

"Sarah has given them fifteen minutes to come up with strategy before agreeing to talk to us," I answered.

"Ah, I see," Tom said and headed to the break room. "I have time for another cup of coffee."

"I'll take one with cream, Tom," Sarah added.

"You sure you want to drink that stuff?" I asked.

"After a while you don't even notice its bad," she said.

I shrugged and went to my desk. I wanted to have my notebook ready along with the file when we were summoned to the interrogation room. I needed my game face on. There was a message to call Eli when I had a minute. I hesitated then decided I should wait until after the interview. I did not want our conversation cut short.

Then Sarah got the invitation from the family lawyer. We could begin our interrogation. I went to the break room to get Tom.

We followed Sarah into the interrogation room. "I'm Assistant District Attorney Sarah Stephens. These are Detectives McVannel and Maxwell. They will be conducting this interview. How much consideration this young lady gets will depend on how honestly she answers their questions. The charges against her are plenty and my office has not decided whether or not to try her as an adult." Sarah turned and left the room.

Tom and I took our seats across the table from Katelyn, her father, and their attorney. I had my notebook ready and the file on the case beside it.

Tom nodded and I asked the first question, "You understand, Katelyn, you are being charged with distribution of pornography of a minor and prostitution?"

Katelyn whose eyes were red from crying, nodded her head in the affirmative.

"For this to go in your favor, we need you to answer questions with your voice. Do you understand?"

"Yes," she mumbled as tears rolled down her cheeks.

Mr. Walker asked, "Is it all right if I give her my hankie?"

"It is," Tom answered. Mr. Walker produced a hankie and gave it to his daughter.

She wiped her eyes and looked first at Tom and then at me and asked listlessly, "What do you want to know?"

"How did you come to be involved with Chelsie Patton and her schemes?" I asked.

Katelyn took a deep breath, "I was new as a freshman, and she saw me as competition for her role as queen bee. I hadn't been in school two weeks, when a photo of me in the locker room showed up in my locker. I was topless getting ready to go to the shower. The note with it said I was to play down my charm and join Chelsie at lunch. I was horrified the photo might get out so I joined Chelsie and her group at lunch. I have bowed to her will ever since."

"You agreed to prostitute yourself as part of her payment to Dustin Bell?" Tom was incredulous.

"He's not so bad. I got used to it after a while. Chelsie would call me and tell me Dustin needed a date and I'd go with him. The agreement was for touching privileges. He kept pushing until it was full sex. I felt trapped," she explained.

"What do you mean you got used to it?" her father bellowed.

"Mr. Walker, you need to calm down," said Guy Smythe the lawyer.

"Your attorney is right, Mr. Walker," I said quietly. "If you can't be quiet, we will have you escorted out."

Mr. Walker looked at both of them, then at his daughter with disgust before rising and walking from the room.

Katelyn whispered, "Daddy," then dissolved into tears.

"Let's get this done," Smythe said firmly.

"What do you know about this photo?" Tom asked passing the photo of Michelle to Katelyn.

Katelyn glanced at it, "Chelsie had that horrid Ellie take it. Dustin put it on his computer and sent it to Chelsie with instructions on how to share it with everyone at school."

"Did you know she was going to send it out?" Tom wanted to know.

"No, she called and asked me to come to her house. When I got there, she handed me an envelope and told me it had to get to Dustin on Friday night. His parents would be out of town for the weekend. Chelsie was my cover and I spent the whole night with Dustin. It was the only time," she ended.

"You didn't figure it out when the photo hit the school on Thursday?" again I was having trouble following her logic.

"I was signed out on Thursday for a dentist appointment. I didn't go back to school until Friday," she said without emotion.

"Do you consider Dustin your boyfriend?" Tom asked.

"NO WAY!" Katelyn's head shot up. "He's okay for sex, but not someone I want to spend time with. He's boring."

"I think we have what we need for now." I told her. "Your attorney will meet you at the court house in an hour for arraignment."

"Will my Dad be there?" she asked.

"We have no control over him, but we will notify him when it is," I told her honestly.

We stood to leave. She would talk a bit with her attorney and then be led back to the holding cell.

Mr. Walker was having a cup of coffee with Sarah Stephens. He seemed to have calmed down.

Tom approached him, "Mr. Walker, may I have a word with you?"

The man rose and followed Tom. Tom led him to the observation room. Walker looked at his daughter as she sobbed.

"She'd like you to be at her arraignment in an hour," Tom said. "My partner is talking to the Assistant District Attorney about charging her as a minor, which means if she keeps herself out of trouble until she is twenty-one, her record will be expunged."

The man looked at Tom, relief written all over his face. "Can I see her?"

"Right this way," Tom said and led him back into the interrogation room.

Joining Sarah and I, Tom asked, "Charging her as a juvenile?"

"I don't see any reason not to, she's a victim," Sarah answered. "See you in court. We have two arraignments today; Dustin Bell for breaking and entering, distribution of pornography via the Internet, and setting up the dummy website which drove Alana Gray to be home schooled, then this young lady, although I will ask the judge to send this one to juvenile court."

"We're going to grab some lunch at Dollie's if you want to join us," Tom said.

"I'll pass this time; I want to have all my paper work in order. Judge Allen has asked to hear all the preliminary cases is this," Sarah answered. "See you in court." She walked out of the office.

Tom and I signed out and headed to Dollie's Deli. Once inside we ordered quickly. Tom a ham and cheese sandwich with tomato, lettuce, and mayonnaise. I had a chicken, spinach salad with raspberry vinaigrette on the side. Tom ordered another cup of coffee and

I asked for iced tea with lemon. After the waitress walked away Tom said, "How does one girl get so many others to do her evil bidding?"

"I know you don't expect me to have an answer," I responded.

"No, anyone who has the answer will make millions," Tom replied. "How do I protect my kids from this?" Tom ran his hands through his hair. I knew from years of working with him he was stressed by this case.

I reached over and grabbed one of his hands forcing him to look at me, "You and Shannon have done a great job with the boys. They know right from wrong. Keep them busy with sports and fishing and they won't have time for this kind of stuff," I told him.

"Somewhere deep inside, I know you're right, Macy. I just feel so bad for some of these kids. The young girl we just interviewed thinks prostituting herself makes what she's done okay. I don't understand," Tom continued.

"There are things we will never understand. Don't beat yourself up anticipating things which may never happen," I assured him.

Our food and drinks arrived and we concentrated on them. After we were done, we paid and headed to the courthouse. It was going to be interesting to see what Judge Allen did with these two.

THE COURTROOM WAS somber. I could see Mr. Walker and his attorney. Mad Miller was also there which meant Dustin Bell was being arraigned today, too. This was going to prove more interesting than I had first thought.

The bailiff entered and announced, "All rise for the Honorable Judge Elizabeth Allen."

Everyone stood as Judge Allen entered and took her seat. She nodded to the bailiff, and asked, "What do we have before us today?"

"First the case of the State of Michigan vs. Katelyn Walker, charged with distribution of pornography of a minor and prostitution."

Katelyn standing next to her attorney at the defense table seemed to shrivel in front of the judge.

"How does the defendant plead?" asked Judge Allen.

"Not guilty, your Honor," her attorney answered.

"I'll hear from the prosecution," the judge stated.

"Your Honor, the prosecution is asking this case be transferred to juvenile court," Sarah said.

"Is she not part of this whole hideous pornography ring at the school?" Judge Allen demanded.

"She is, your Honor, however the prosecution believes the best interests of everyone would be served in juvenile court," Sarah shot back.

"Mr. Smythe?" the judge asked.

"We concur, your Honor," he responded.

"So ordered. Ms. Stephens, your office will keep me apprised of how this case turns out," she said.

"Yes, your Honor."

The gavel banged. Katelyn was led out. Mr. Walker joined Mr. Smythe and the two of them left the room.

"Next case," the judge said.

"The State of Michigan vs Dustin Bell, one count breaking and entering, one count of illegal use of a computer, and one count contributing to the delinquency of a minor," the bailiff read the charges.

Dustin stood with Mad Miller at the defense table.

"How does the defendant plead?" the judge asked.

"Not guilty," Dustin answered.

"Prosecution?"

Sarah stood up and began, "Mr. Bell was caught breaking into the home of Detective Sergeant Macy McVannel. He was on an errand for Chelsie Patton. He received pay for this in cash and sex with a minor child. We seek to try him as an adult."

The judge glared at Dustin. He did not even flinch. "Young man, how old are you?"

"I am nineteen, your Honor," he responded almost defiantly.

"And what was the age of the girl when you first had sex with her?" the judge demanded.

Mad Miller objected, "My client has been advised to plead the fifth on this."

"Remand this young man over to superior court to be tried as an adult," she said and added to Sarah, "Go easy on the young woman." Then her gavel came down.

TOM AND I had the information we needed. Now we had to do something about the Ellie Wexford situation. She was still in custody, but had not been arraigned. It was time to find her mother or other family. We were still looking for her father.

A caseworker from child services was waiting for us. "I'm Martha Daly, I heard you need information on Ellie Wexford?" she began.

"We need to know how she ended up with a father who'd been jailed for taking nude photos of her when she was a toddler," I said disgustedly.

"Is there someplace we can talk?" she asked.

"This way," I said heading to the interrogation room.

"Ms. Daly, would you like coffee?" Tom asked.

She looked at him to see if he was kidding, and then shook her head no. She followed me and Tom came behind us.

Once inside I offered her a seat. Tom had grabbed the notebook, which told me he did not want to talk to this woman.

"I'm waiting to learn how this happened, Ms. Daly?" I said impatiently.

I had remained standing, mostly because this situation angered me, but also hoping Ms. Daly would find it intimidating. I paced waiting for her to explain.

"Detective, we didn't place her there. Her mother died and no one else would take her. What choice did we have?" she asked. "Our job is to keep families together."

"A father who uses his daughter in pornographic photos is a family?" I exploded letting out all my frustration. "What kind of life is that for a child?"

"Her father did five years for his crime. He'd been rehabilitated and had gainful employment. The child had no one else," Ms. Daly said as if she were reading a case file.

"How old was she when she went to live with him?" I asked.

"She had just turned eight," responded Ms. Daly as if it excused the lack of follow-up.

"And what was the gainful employment?" I continued.

"Let's see," she flipped some pages in her file, "ah here it is. He was a stock person at a local warehouse." She looked pleased with herself.

"He's no longer a stock person. Were you aware he's now a long haul truck driver? He is rarely home?" I kept hammering at her.

"No, we had no reason to keep checking," she defended her department.

"No *reason*!" I was outraged. "You have no way of knowing whether or not she was used as a teen in pornographic photos? Or for prostitution?"

"We kept tabs on the family for a year," she said quietly. "We have no obligation beyond the year. We had no complaints from the neighbors."

"Have you ever been to the dump she lives in?" I asked.

"Well, no of course not," Ms. Daly became indignant.

"She is eating fast food and drinking. No one has cleaned house in months. She skips school whenever she feels like going off with her camera," I was close to shouting. "No one has looked after this child for years. Would it surprise you, she is being charged with taking pornographic photos?" I put both hands on the table and leaned into her face. "Yet you had no obligation." I turned and left the room.

Ms. Daly handed Tom a type written report she had brought with her and flounced from the room and out of the station.

Tom joined me in the break room. "Macy, are you okay?

"I'm fine. I just don't understand bureaucrats," I told him. I was still pacing.

"Let's read through this stuff and have a conversation with Sarah. Maybe there's some way to get her a break," Tom suggested.

I took the offered file from him and returned to my desk. The system had sure done nothing for Ellie Wexford so far, maybe we could change it.

CHAPTER EIGHTEEN

The next few hours were spent going over the Wexford file, trying to locate anyone who could tell us where her father was. Chase Wexford had fallen off the map. Finally I did a computer search to see if he had been incarcerated somewhere. A file popped up saying Wexford had been arrested in a small town in Kansas after posing as a talent scout and taking nude photos of a couple of young girls. He was held over for arraignment in the local jail and had died mysteriously in the night. This had taken place when Ellie was sixteen.

"Oh, my god, Tom!" I gasped. "Ellie Wexford has been fending for herself for two years at least."

"What did you find?" he asked.

"Chase Wexford was arrested in Kansas for pornography and died in his cell before he could be arraigned," I answered. "It happened when Ellie was about sixteen."

"No wonder the place is a dump. Do you think she knows?" he asked.

"I don't know, but I think we need to talk to her," I told him as the printout came off my printer.

Tom and I headed for the detention center Ellie was being held in.

"Warden Crayton this is Macy McVannel," I said into my cell phone.

"One moment, please," and I was put on hold.

"Detective McVannel, this is Alice Crayton, how may I help you?" she asked answering the phone.

"Ellie Wexford, something has come up in regard to her. My partner and I are on our way over to talk to her," I told her.

"We'll have her waiting," was the reply.

I hung up the phone saying, "She'll be waiting."

Tom drove to Last Chance Center the juvenile facility we had placed Ellie in. He was thoughtful most of the trip as we pulled in the driveway he said, "We have to help her somehow, Macy."

I looked sideways at Tom, "I know. Let's see what she knows first."

We entered, signed in, and gave our weapons to the officer of the day. We were led through a gate which clanged loudly as it closed behind us. The officer led us through a doorway into a library. Ellie was seated at the window with a sketch book. She looked up when we came in.

"They didn't tell me it was you," she said disgustedly.

"We've been doing some checking on your father," I started."

She glanced up quickly then back down at her sketch book, "Is he coming?"

"Ellie," I began, "why didn't you tell us he's been missing for two years?"

She gave a harsh laugh, "So you could lock me up in a place like this? Or worse yet, send me to foster care?"

"We found out what happened to your dad," I said.

Ellie stared at me, "What do you mean, what happened to him?"

"It seems he was arrested in Kansas a couple of years ago and charged with taking pornographic photos. He died before he could be arraigned," I told her watching for a change in expression.

Tears formed in her eyes and she wiped them with her hands. "How did he die?"

"I don't know. The report says he died in his sleep," I told her honestly.

"You mean someone in the jail killed him for what he'd done," she stated.

"I don't know for sure."

Tom was looking at the books on the shelf ignoring the two of us. I do not know what kind of reaction he expected but I could sense he was ready if needed.

"So, I'm stuck here then?" Ellie asked.

"Detective Maxwell and I are working on it. We'd both like to see your photography talent put to good use. First, you have to be honest with me about your work for Chelsie," I told her.

"I started taking photos for the drama queen because she offered to pay me money. I didn't know where my dad was and I wanted to be there when he came home," she said flatly. "Then it became a challenge to see if I could get shots in places where no one expected to have pictures taken. I kept the negatives so Chelsie wouldn't welch on the deal. If you look through them carefully, there are a couple shots of her; she wouldn't want to get out." The smug look on her face told me Chelsie did not know about this.

"We are going to have to find you a place to stay before we can spring you," I told her. "It won't be a foster home as you are eighteen. It will be somewhere people will expect you to finish school and apply to a college. This will hang over your head until the college is completed and you are gainfully employed."

She shrugged. "I've been learning to draw so I have it to work on, too."

"May I see what you've done?" Tom asked holding a hand out for her sketch book.

Ellie hesitated then asked, "Is this another trick?"

Tom laughed, "No, I'd really like to see what you're doing."

Reluctantly she handed him the sketchbook. He slowly flipped through the pages. Handing it back to her, he said, "You have quite a bit of talent."

Ellie blushed as she took the book back. "Thank you," she mumbled.

Tom took out a business card and handed it to Ellie saying, "If you need anything call me or ask for Detective McVannel. We'll see you as soon as we have something worked out."

She took the card and put it in her pocket. As Tom and I left the room, I heard her sobbing. *Rotten as he might have been, he was her father and she had held out hope he would return.*

"WHAT ARE WE going to do for her?" Tom asked as we drove back to the station.

"Talk to Sarah Stephens, we need to find her a place to live. She's too old to be fostered. But it needs to be someplace where she has chores and it is expected she'll attend school," I told him. "Her grades from the sheet Mrs. Sweeny gave us show she's kept her grades up."

"Well, there's a plus," Tom said. "I'd offer to take her in, but with the baby, Shannon would kill me."

"She can't stay with me. I have enough things to work out in my own life to take responsibility for someone else's," I told him frankly.

"Things not going well with Eli?" asked Tom.

"Eli isn't a problem," I said sharply.

Tom looked sideways at me, "Sorry, Macy, I didn't mean to pry."

I laughed. "It's not anything. We are getting to know each other is all."

"Glad to know." Tom focused on the road ahead and was silent.

I WALKED TO my desk grabbed all the files and looked at Tom, "We need a board." Then I headed for our conference room.

Tom grabbed a cup of coffee and joined me. "Why do we need a board?"

"I need to get a handle on who did what. I think we have more victims than criminals," I told him. "For instance, Katelyn is going to be charged with prostitution and yet she was blackmailed into using her body."

"She could have said, no," Tom reasoned.

"Then she'd be in the hospital, home-schooled, or have moved out of town," I retorted.

"Okay, I see your point," Tom said reluctantly.

The first picture up was Chelsie Patton. She was the center connecting all of them. Then came her best friend Abby Stark followed by her other best friend Katelyn Walker. Next, we have Dustin Bell and Ellie Wexford. Finally, we have Matt Alexander, Alana Grey, and Michelle Watson. I put spaces for Mary Golden, Tansy Taylor, and Mr. Blackstone. I believed they too, were victims of Chelsie Patton.

"How does this play out now?" Tom asked.

"I'm not sure. I think we need to find Mary Golden, Tansy Taylor, and Mr. Blackstone," I said. "Looks like I know where to start the next phase."

"Time to call it a day, Macy," Tom said. "You're going to make yourself sick over this."

"And all this time I've been worried about you," I chuckled. "Okay, let's call it a day."

We left the board and put the files back on my desk. It was time to go talk to Eli.

CHAPTER NINETEEN

I called Eli from my cell on the drive home, "Hello."

"Hi, Eli, do you need me to pick up anything on my way home?" I asked.

"Nope, JJ took me shopping. Meet me on the deck," his excitement was barely concealed.

"What's going on?" was my suspicious response.

He hesitated then said, "Not a thing. I'm grilling."

"Okay, I'll be home soon." I shut the phone thinking, *he's up to something.* I turned on the radio and drove the rest of the way home.

I found Eli at the grill on my deck. He and JJ had cleaned off my deck furniture and the table was beautifully set under a new umbrella. The biggest surprise was the new hot tub.

"My, my you have been busy today," I said stepping onto the deck.

"I thought you could use some relaxation," Eli said grinning.

The food on the grill smelled delicious. Eli had wine chilling and poured me a glass. I took it and looked at my yard admiring the work done today.

"So I thought JJ was becoming a farmer, how did you guys get this and the door all done in one day?" I asked.

"It was simple, we hired people to help," he said honestly. "I'm still a bit of a gimp if you will remember."

I chuckled. This felt good. Coming home to Eli and dinner was great; the hot tub was a bonus.

"You know, a girl could get mighty used to this," I told him, then watched his reaction over the rim of my glass.

"I'm glad to hear you say so, Macy," he answered smiling.

We had a wonderful dinner of steak, salad, and roasted corn on the cob. As the sun set we put on our swim suits and slipped into the hot tub to watch the stars come out and finish our bottle of wine. As I leaned into Eli and watched the heavens, I knew this was where I should be.

"Can you tell me about the case?" he asked quietly.

"It's awful. Kids tormenting kids is the worst. One girl is in the hospital, one is being homeschooled, and we are tracking down two others. I don't know how one person can gain so much hold over others and get them to do her evil," I told him.

"Kids have always picked on other kids," Eli said as he held me tighter.

"We didn't have cell phones, Internet, and all the other things kids do today. We also never intended another kid would be harmed because of what we did," I answered seriously. "I know what it feels like to be picked on. This is beyond anything we ever did."

"Let it go tonight, Macy," Eli said and turned me in his arms for a kiss.

I melted into him as the kiss deepened not wanting anything to intrude on the moment. I knew I was falling in love with him.

Thursday

Morning came too early. I could hear Eli in the kitchen. Rolling out of bed, I grabbed the tea sitting on my nightstand and took it with me to the bathroom. After my workout, and shower I went to the kitchen where Eli was just putting breakfast on the table.

"So, what are your big plans for the day?" I asked sitting down to dig in.

"JJ is picking me up at ten and I'm going to the doctor for a check-up," he answered. "Then I'm going to see my captain about returning to work."

I felt myself stiffen. Returning to work, meant putting himself in harms' way. It meant I was going to risk losing him every day. Focusing on my breakfast, I asked, "Are we doing anything special for dinner?"

"Do you want to?" he asked watching me closely.

"I really hadn't thought about it," was my honest answer. *What I wanted was to not think about Eli going back to work.*

"How about I stop in and see if you can have lunch with me? We can talk about it then," he suggested.

"Sure, sounds like a good plan," I answered. When breakfast was over I took my dishes to the sink, Eli came up behind me.

"Macy, I'm going to be okay," he said as he wrapped his arms around me.

"I know," I said flippantly.

"You don't know, and which is what has you scared," he answered as though reading my thoughts. "It's okay to be scared." He turned me and kissed me passionately. "Now get off to work, before Tom sends a search party," he chuckled handing me my bag as I strapped on my gun.

I left smiling. *If he said it would be okay, I'd take his word for it.* I put it out of my mind and set off for work.

MY PHONE RANG as I was driving to work. I picked it up saying, "Hello."

"Macy, where are you?" Tom asked urgently.

"On my way in, thought I'd stop at the hospital and check on Michelle Watson," I responded.

"Good idea, then get here quick we have a lead on Tansy Taylor," he told me.

"I should be there in about twenty minutes," I told him and hung up. *Wonder what has him so anxious this morning?*

Pulling into the hospital, I parked and headed for the intensive care unit. I stopped at the nurses' station and showed my ID. One of the nurses whose name tag read Patsy said, "Will you come with me please?"

I followed her to a small waiting room. She motioned me to sit down and she sat.

"Mrs. Watson gave us permission to give you Michelle's medical information," she started. "Michelle is showing signs of coming out of the coma. At this time we do not know if there is any brain damage."

"Thank you. I'm glad to hear she's coming around," I said. "However I get a feeling there is a 'but' here."

"You are very perceptive, Detective McVannel," she said. "So far, Michelle is not reacting to pain stimuli in her extremities."

"What exactly are you telling me?" I asked.

"It means she does not appear to have feeling in her feet and legs," she responded. "She may have paralysis."

I handed her my card and said, "Will you call me when she regains consciousness? I need to speak to her."

"Someone will," she said, "I'll attach your card to her chart with a notation to call you."

I stood, shook her hand, and left the room. As I walked to my car, I pondered what it all meant for the sixteen year old lying in a hospital bed.

TOM WAS IN the break room with a cup of coffee when I arrived. He saw me and came to my desk. "Let's go look at the board." He grabbed a file and headed to the conference room.

"Okay," I said catching up to him. "What gives?"

"First, I've tracked down Tansy Taylor. She is in a mental ward downstate. It seems she had a break down and the family moved away before it could get out," he told me.

"Any chance of talking to her parents?" I asked.

"Her parents live near the private hospital she's in," he answered. "I left a message for them to call me."

"Well, I have some news on Michelle," I told him. "She is starting to come out of her coma."

"Sounds like a good thing," Tom said excitedly.

"Maybe and maybe not," I replied. "The nurse says she's not responding to pain stimuli in her legs and feet."

"What are you saying, Macy?" Tom's facial expression went from happiness to anger in a fleeting second.

"She may have some paralysis." I stated bluntly. "Do we have any leads on Mary Golden?"

"I'm waiting to hear something," his forlorn look told me he was not holding out much hope.

"Well, let's see if we can find out what happened to cause Tansy to breakdown," I suggested.

We headed back to our desks. Tom went on the computer to search for any articles which might explain how Tansy Taylor had ended up in a private mental ward. I started a second search on Mary Golden. I also did some paperwork on the students we had already interviewed and or arrested.

I had also put in a call to a friend at child welfare to see what could be done for Ellie Wexford. I was determined to save at least one child from the mess Chelsie Patton had created.

My mind was filled with the case at hand and I was surprised when Eli showed up with a bouquet of flowers. Whistles came from my co-workers when he entered and headed toward my desk. I smiled as he approached trying to ignore the blush creeping up my neck and onto my cheeks.

Eli handed me the flowers and looked at Tom, "Can I steal your partner for lunch?"

"Sure, I can reach her on her cell if something breaks," Tom smiled at me as he answered. "Macy, I think there's a vase in the break room for your flowers."

I took the hint and headed to the break room to put my flowers in water. Wondering, *what are those two up to now?* Eli and Tom were shaking hands as I made my way toward them. I put the flowers on my desk, reached for my purse, and left with Eli before anyone else could ask questions.

"Where are we off to?" I asked.

"I have a limo downstairs, we are dining in style," he responded.

Right outside was a black limo complete with driver waiting to whisk us away. Eli and I slid into the back seat. The driver closed the door and went around getting behind the wheel and driving away.

Eli took me in his arms and kissed me as though we had been apart for weeks. When we finally came up for air, I laughed. "Care to tell me what this is all about?"

"We are celebrating," he told me. "I had taken the captain's exam two weeks before I took the protection detail at the Appleton farm. I passed."

I was stunned. He had said nothing about taking the exam. "I'm happy for you," I said kissing him again.

"So, when I got an all clear from the doctor for a limited return to work, I went to see my captain," Eli said with all seriousness. "I can't be a house boy forever you know."

I pulled out of his arms. Something was telling me I was not going to like the rest of what he had to say.

He held up a hand for silence, "Before you protest, I have a desk job. I'm being put in charge of the missing child division. I won't be out on the streets every day. I do love you, Macy and I want to be around for a very long time to show you how much."

The breath I was holding came out in a gasp, "You took a desk job for me?"

He nodded. "I'd do anything to show you how much you mean to me."

Tears of joy ran down my face, "Eli, I hardly know what to say."

"Don't say anything, just kiss me," he said as his lips closed on mine.

The limo pulled up in front of the beautiful Heritage Inn an old mansion they had turned into an exclusive dining establishment with rooms overlooking the grounds. Our driver let us out and we were escorted to a private dining room. Champagne was on ice and servers discreetly appeared with salads, one poured us each a flute of champagne. Each course came with as little fanfare as possible. Eli and I spent an hour over lunch and walking in the lovely gardens surrounding the inn. We were in the limo returning to town when my cell phone rang.

I saw it was Tom and answered, "McVannel."

"Are you close to the hospital?"

Glancing out the window, I saw we were blocks from the hospital and answered, "Yes, has something happened?"

"Michelle Watson is awake."

"I'll go there now, will you meet me?" I asked.

"On my way as soon as I hang up," he answered.

Closing the phone I looked at Eli, "I'm sorry, but I need to go to the hospital. Our victim is awake."

Eli tapped on the window and gave the driver the new directions. When we rolled into the parking lot at the hospital, Eli asked, "Dinner on the grill and the hot tub tonight?"

"Sounds wonderful," I said smiling as I kissed him goodbye.

CHAPTER TWENTY

There was an unexpected hush in the ICU when I entered. I showed my ID to the desk clerk saying, "My partner, Tom Maxwell will be here any minute. Will we be able to speak to Michelle Watson?"

The clerk gave me a blank look and said, "One moment." She picked up the phone and spoke into it, "A detective is here and wants to talk to Michelle Watson." She listened then answered, "Yes, Ma'am." She hung up the phone and said, "Please come with me." She led the way to the same conference room I had been in earlier. "I'll bring your partner here then the doctor will join you." She left without waiting for me to respond.

My mind was running on overtime, *What was going on? Had Michelle taken a turn for the worst?* I paced the room until I heard the door open. Tom entered.

"I thought you said she was awake," I started.

Tom held up his hand, "I don't know any more than you do. They called just before I called you."

"What did they say?" I asked anxiously.

"Only Michelle Watson was awake and we should come to the hospital," Tom answered. "I have no idea what's going on." He took a seat, I remained standing and we waited.

It was another five minutes before anyone entered the room. A young woman came in saying, "Are you the detectives?"

"Yes," Tom answered standing.

"Please have a seat," she said indicating we should sit. She sat before continuing. "I am Doctor Ava Garcia. The nursing staff called you on my orders. For all intents and purposes Michelle Watson is awake."

"Meaning what exactly?" I asked suspiciously.

"Her eyes are open, she is tracking people by their voices and items with her eyes," Dr. Garcia stated, "however; she is unable to speak."

"Do you know when she might be able to talk?" Tom asked.

"There is no way to tell. We will have to run some tests to determine how much brain damage there is and if it is permanent," she told us.

"Talking to her at this time would be pointless," I said feeling frustrated.

"I'm afraid so, Detective," she answered.

"Please keep us up to date on her progress," Tom said. He stood and held his hand to the doctor.

"We will," she assured him as she took his hand.

I too stood and shook her hand and she was gone. "What do we do now?" I asked.

"Find out exactly what happened to Tansy Taylor," Tom replied. He held the door open and we walked out and down to the parking lot.

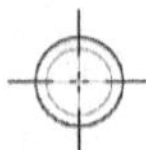

IN THE OFFICE, I found a new folder on my desk. The file request on Mary Golden was in. I opened it and sat abruptly in my chair. "Tom," I said quietly. "We have a problem."

Tom looked at me and said anxiously, "Macy, what is it?"

I handed him the file. I had felt the color drain from my face when I read it. Now I watched Tom have the same reaction. Mary Golden was dead. She had killed herself a month after leaving Rivers Edge. Details of her death were included in the file.

"We need to talk to her parents," Tom said. "They might be able to tell us what was going on with Mary."

"Could Chelsie have caused a death?" I asked incredulously. "This girl is the epitome of evil."

"We won't know until we talk to Mr. and Mrs. Golden," Tom said. "I'll make some calls."

"Tom, are you sure the Goldens will want to talk about it?" I queried.

"I'm calling the police department who handled it first. I want to see if they have anything," he answered me.

Feeling this was spiraling out of our control quickly, I looked again at the photos of Mary Golden in life and Mary Golden in death. *How do kids drive each other to this end? What had Chelsie Patton done to this girl? What had she done to Tansy Taylor?* Needing to walk, I went to the conference room to look at our board. *They all looked like wholesome teens. How did it get this messed up? Were there others we didn't know about? Would this case bring it to an end? How did Chelsie Patton destroy so many and why?* These were questions we would probably never have answers to, but one thing was for certain, Chelsie Patton was the center of a crime spree which had been going on for years.

I was so focused on the board I did not hear the door open. Captain Wellington's voice startled me, "McVannel?"

Turning I answered, "Yes, sir."

"This case is not as easy as you first thought, eh?" he chuckled.

"Nothing involving kids is ever easy, sir," was my response. "Did you need me for something?"

"Just checking to see how you're holding up," he replied.

"Aside from being horrified because kids do this to each other, it's just another case, sir," I told him.

"How's Maxwell?" Wellington asked.

"Holding up well, sir," I answered. "I was worried to begin with, because he has kids of his own, but he's fine."

"Good to know. Carry on," he said and left.

I spent very little time wondering about the captain and his questions. He had every reason to worry I might fall apart, but Tom, never. I turned back to the board trying to find answers not there.

Tom joined me a few minutes later with a handful of printouts. "What's with all the paper?" I asked.

"They faxed us everything on the Mary Golden case and are sending a messenger to deliver her diary," he answered handing me part of the papers. "I made you a copy."

We sat at the table reading through the interviews with the parents and friends of Mary Golden. I was shaking my head at the waste of human life. Everything in her school transcripts said Mary Golden was an honor student. The contradiction came from her friends. She would be reluctant to date, yet had been asked out many times. She was a great athlete, but waited until everyone else had showered before she did. She did not attend sleepovers, but had been asked. She was kind to everyone and volunteered at a nursing home two nights a week after school. Teachers thought she was shy but she never seemed to have trouble with anyone. She was the first to stick up for the underdog. No one had expected her to commit suicide.

"How did she hide her feelings so well?" Tom asked. "Didn't anyone see she was in trouble?"

"Kids are great at putting on an appearance for the public," I answered. "Look at Chelsie Patton; she believed she was invincible even when we took her out of the school in hand cuffs."

Tom nodded, "I can't wait for a look at her diary. I wonder if it will give us a clue?"

"It's late," I said looking at the clock. "Eli and I are going to celebrate his promotion tonight."

"Yeah," he said distractedly. "You go on. I'm going to read this again and see if something leaps out at me."

I left him in the conference room trying to make sense out of something which did not make sense. Putting my files on my desk so they would be at the ready in the morning, I grabbed my purse, and headed toward the exit.

CHAPTER
TWENTY-ONE

I was looking forward to the evening with Eli. Dinner would be spectacular even if he only grilled hamburger. Watching the stars in his arms in the hot tub would also be wonderful. I knew I was falling love with him and I would have to tell him soon. The gnawing sense something would happen if I did would not leave me. I'd lost two men to the job, first my father, then my finance'. Losing another would send me over the edge.

Eli was on the deck and sure enough, hamburgers were on the grill. He also had veggie kabobs ready to go on and a salad. He poured a glass of wine and brought it to me. "Was today any better?" he asked hugging me.

"It is now," I told him returning his hug as I took the glass of wine. "Our victim is alive but cannot speak or move. They are running tests to see how much damage has been done."

"Not good," he said. I could see him frowning.

"We have information on two other girls who were also victimized. One is in a private mental hospital and the other killed herself. I still don't understand what drives one person to hurt so many," I told him pondering my thoughts on Chelsie Patton again. "Dinner smells delicious."

Eli picked up my change of subject, "Well, it's not the Heritage Inn, but I make do."

We both chuckled and I wrapped my arms around his waist. He took the wine glass from me and turned to kiss me. "Macy, we need to talk about us."

"I know," I murmured. I snuggled into his chest, "After dinner, please. I'm starved."

Laughing Eli let me go and served our dinner. We talked about our friends and his promotion while we ate and cleaned up. Heavy conversation would come later while we sat in the hot tub.

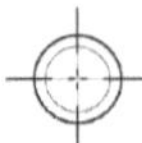

AS I LEANED back in Eli's arms to watch the stars, he said quietly, "I think it's time I move back to my apartment."

I stiffened, "If it's what you want."

"Macy, what I want is to marry you and spend the rest of my life with you," he answered holding me tighter. "This was just temporary. We knew it when I moved in. I'm not leaving you, I'm just leaving temptation. Besides, I start work on Monday."

"When were you planning to tell me?" I asked annoyed. I was more annoyed with myself than with Eli. *How long did I really think we could continue playing house anyway?*

"I only found out today," he answered.

"Do you plan to go with me on Sunday to Mimi's baptism?" I asked.

"Unless you don't want me too," he replied. "I was hoping we'd go from there to your niece's graduation party. I want to meet your family, Macy."

I turned so I could face him and set my glass on the rim of the tub. "I want more than anything to spend Sunday with you and my family," I told him in earnest. Then before he could say anything else, I kissed him. Telling him with actions, what I could not yet bring myself to say in words.

Eli pulled away looking closely at my face, "I'll wait for as long as you want."

"I know," I told him leaning my head on his chest.

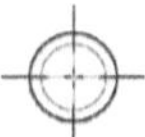

Friday

I was up early and in the shower when I heard Eli moving around. I finished getting dressed and headed for the kitchen. This morning I was planning to make breakfast. I had put the coffee on when I first got up so it would be ready. I squeezed some orange juice and started making omelets. Eli joined me within a few minutes.

"Good morning, sunshine," he greeted me. "What's with the breakfast?

"It's my turn," I said smiling. I turned to him for a kiss and was whisked off my feet. "Good morning, to you too," I laughed as he set me back down and started getting out dishes.

As I finished the eggs, Eli made toast and was putting it on the table. "So, I tell you I'm moving back home and this is my send off?"

"Never," I poked him with my elbow as I set his plate in front of him. "Breakfast is the one meal I can cook and it really is my turn." I sat and started to eat.

"Okay, do you want to come to my apartment for dinner?" he asked.

"We could do something wild and crazy like going out," I countered.

"How about I check with you at lunch time and we decide then?"

"I'm all for it," I said taking a drink of orange juice.

"I have clean up. You have a case to solve," he told me collecting our plates. He turned after putting the dishes in the sink to take me in his arms. As he kissed me with more passion than I had ever dreamed, I felt myself melting into him. "Be safe today, Macy."

I walked to my car in a daze. *No doubt about it, I was head over heels in love with Eli. Why, why couldn't I bring myself to tell him?* As I pulled myself together so I could drive to work, Eli was not far from my mind.

TOM WAS AT his desk studying something when I walked in. He did not even look up. I had no messages so I headed to the break room where I filled Tom's cup with coffee and grabbed a bottle of water for myself. Returning to our desks, I set the cup on his and sat down reaching for last night's file.

"Macy, Chelsie Patton is a sociopath," Tom said without looking up.

"What brings you to that conclusion?" I asked frowning.

"This is Mary Golden's diary," he said holding up what he was reading. "She chronicled Chelsie's actions leading to her committing suicide. It's so very sad."

"It just goes to show there is a pattern to Chelsie's behavior," I agreed. "And it will make the prosecution's case stronger."

"If we can get it admitted," Tom's voice sounded doubtful. "You know prior bad acts."

"But if this establishes a pattern and Matt Alexander and Alana Grey testify," I started "there should be no problem."

"We'll see. I want you to read this I'm almost done," he answered.

I went back to yesterday's information and tried to make sense of it. We learned Mary Golden had killed herself and Tansy Taylor was in a private hospital. We did not know what the issues were with Tansy, but my guess was it could be laid at Chelsie's door, too. The girl is just bad news.

Tom finished reading, handed me the diary, picked up his cup, and said, "I'm going for a walk." Without any other comment, he left the room. I watched as he took the cup to the break room, then stopped at the front desk and left the building.

I reached for the diary thinking, *This must be some heavy duty stuff.* I opened the book and began to read. I was so engrossed in the diary I did not see Tom return. He set a cup of tea on my desk before sitting at his. I nodded my thanks and kept reading. When I finished a few minutes later, I looked at him and said, "We really have to talk to Tansy Taylor's parents."

"I called them when I came in this morning," he answered. "I just picked up a message to call them back."

"Don't waste time," I said urgently. "We need to know if Tansy also kept a diary."

"We have a lot of questions to ask them and it won't be easy," Tom agreed reaching for the phone.

I stood and stretched taking my tea to the break room, while he made the call. *Tom was right, Chelsie Patton was a sociopath. She had to be stopped before anyone else was hurt. How did she get this way? The girl had it all, money, looks, intelligence, parents who indulged her every whim, and a mind twisted so badly it had no morals.*

Tom entered the break room saying, "We have an appointment with the Taylors in an hour. Are you ready to go?"

"Sure, am."

I grabbed my purse, the file we had been using and we headed for the car. Tom chose to drive. I pulled out my notebook and wrote some preliminary questions. "Who's asking questions?" I wanted to know.

"Let's play it by ear," Tom suggested.

"Sounds good." I continued with possible questions, knowing questions would come out of our conversation with the Taylors, too.

It took us almost the full hour to reach the Taylor home. It was a modest house in a subdivision of modest homes. The yard was well tended but it did not have a welcome feeling. It was more a forlorn, melancholy type of feeling I had as we approached the house.

Mr. Taylor was at the door when we came up the steps. "Detectives?"

"I'm Detective Tom Maxwell and this is my partner, Detective Sgt. Macy McVannel."

"Please come in. My wife is getting us some lemonade. Do you mind if we talk on the deck?" he asked leading the way through the house to the deck. "Please, please sit down."

Mrs. Taylor joined us with a pitcher of lemonade and four glasses. As we sat, she began to pour handing each of us a glass.

"I know this will be difficult," Tom started. "We'd like to ask you about your daughter, Tansy."

"Anything we can do to help," Mr. Taylor said. He reached for his wife's hand.

"Can you tell us about Tansy?" I asked.

Mrs. Taylor smiled, "Tansy is beautiful in an ethereal sense. She was a dancer. It was her dream."

"What happened?" Tom asked.

"She started seeing Matt Alexander two years ago," Mrs. Taylor told us. "He was such a nice boy. Then the phone calls started coming. First, it was heavy breathing then they said nasty things to Tansy. Finally, she just wouldn't answer the phone." Mrs. Taylor hung her head.

Mr. Taylor took up the story, "We thought it was kids' pranks, but we notified the phone company. They told us there was nothing they could do. We felt so helpless."

"Did you talk to anyone at the school?" I asked.

"Tansy went to see the counselor, but it just seemed to make things worse," Mrs. Taylor said her face reflecting her memory of the time. "Then those horrible pictures showed up."

"What pictures?" Tom wanted to know.

"Someone put Tansy's face on naked dancers," her father answered. "At first she laughed it off. Later when she was getting ready for her recital, the photos got worse. It was just too much for her." Tears filled his eyes.

"How did Tansy cope with it?" I asked trying to get to what had happened.

"Tansy was ready for her recital and a messenger showed up with flowers and another photo. It showed Tansy's face on a naked woman dancing with a pole," her mother said through her tears. "It wasn't Tansy's body, we knew. She danced in the recital like, she had never danced before. Afterward, when we had all gone to bed, she took some pills and drank whiskey from her father's cabinet." She cried freely dabbing at her face with a handkerchief.

Mr. Taylor took up the story, "I found her in the den when I came down in the morning. I couldn't wake her and called 9-1-1. By the time the ambulance arrived I'd found a pill bottle. There were still some in it so they could identify what she took." He took a deep breath. "It was some kind of amphetamine and mixed with the whiskey, it took her senses away." His wife patted his arm.

"We don't have alcohol in the house anymore," she told us. "I keep telling him it wasn't his fault."

"It wasn't your fault," I agreed. "Do you still have any of the photos she received?"

Mrs. Taylor stared at me, "We put them away. The local police weren't interested in them. Give me a minute." She stood and went inside.

"I wanted to get rid of them," Mr. Taylor told us. "I thought they were just a bad reminder of what happened to our Tansy."

Tom empathized by saying, "I understand. I have a daughter of my own."

"I'm so glad you kept them," I told him. "We think we know who was behind them and we'd like to bring them to justice."

He nodded, wiping his eyes, "It won't bring my Tansy back."

"No, it won't, Mr. Taylor," I said, "but it will prevent some other young girl from taking the drastic steps Tansy did."

"Has someone been hurt?" he asked.

"Yes," I said bluntly. "Two others, one young woman died by her own hand and one is in the hospital."

"Oh my God," he cried. "We should have pushed the police harder. Instead, we just moved away."

"It's not your fault," Tom assured him. "No one could have predicted this would happen again. I think Tansy was an experiment and things have escalated since then."

"I didn't think anything could be worse," he replied. "No one should outlive their children."

Mrs. Taylor returned and handed me a file, "Please don't open them here."

I nodded respecting her wishes. "Thank you for your time. I think we have everything we need."

"Don't bring those back," she said. "I no longer need the reminders."

"As you wish," I said.

Tom and I rose, shook hands with both the Taylors, and left via a fence in the backyard. I did not open the folder in the car either.

"I can't imagine how they must feel," Tom's seriousness told me he was thinking how he would feel if it were Mimi or the boys who had been bullied.

Not knowing how to answer, I chose to say nothing. When we arrived at the police station, I headed to the conference room. Tom stopped for a cup of coffee and brought me a cup of tea. I had the file from the Taylors open in front of me.

"How bad is it?" he asked handing me the cup.

"Pretty much classic Chelsie," I told him. "They are disgusting and I could see how they would upset Tansy."

"Wait," Tom said excitedly, "what's written on the back?"

I turned over the photo I was holding. The words on the back read: 'Everyone will know what you are.'

"Do you think this is Chelsie's writing?" I asked thinking *finally we have something she actually did.*

"I hope so," Tom grinned. "Let's see if we can get her to write those words for us."

"She's been released to her parents," I reminded him. "They won't let us anywhere near her."

"We have to talk to Sarah anyway so we'll ask her to get the sample," Tom smirked.

"Make the call."

He dialed Sarah from the conference room phone. "Tom Maxwell for Sarah Stephens," he said.

"Sarah, Macy and I need you to get a writing sample from Chelsie Patton.

"She needs to write: 'Everyone will know what you are.' We have something for comparison," his voice sounded almost eager.

"Yes, we have done some follow up and see a pattern. Thanks," he finished and hung up the phone. To me he said, "She's going to see if she can get them in this afternoon. We need to get these photos and the diary ready for her to see."

I took the photos and placed them in the folder. Then I headed for the lab. I wanted to know if we would be able to get any fingerprints off them.

ELI CALLED WHILE I was on my way back from the lab, "Macy, have you thought about dinner?"

"I'm sorry, we got a lead, and I completely forgot," I replied.

"No problem. I'll make us some reservations and pick you about seven-thirty," he told me cheerfully.

"I'll be ready." *More than ready I was thinking as I remembered this morning's kiss.*

Tom met me in the hallway, "Sarah has a time lined up to get a handwriting sample." I saw his eagerness but sensed there was more. "The hospital called, grab your stuff, Michelle is talking."

Quickly going to my desk for my purse, I followed in Tom's wake as he headed for the car. We rode in silence to the hospital.

IN THE ICU, Tom and I stopped at the nurses' station. "Detectives Maxwell and McVannel," Tom said to the clerk. "We were called about Michelle Watson."

"Right this way," she said getting up and leading us to a patient room.

Mrs. Watson glanced our way, "Thank you for coming," she said.

"Is Michelle able to talk to us?" I asked.

Mrs. Watson squeezed Michelle's hand, "I'll be right back."

Michelle watched her mother as she walked toward us. We stepped into the hallway to allow Mrs. Watson to come out. She led the way to an empty waiting room.

"I told the nurses to call you," she said. "Michelle cannot speak, but she can nod her head yes and no. If you can ask her yes or no questions, she can answer."

Tom shook his head, "Will she regain her voice?"

"Honestly," Mrs. Watson said, "we have no idea. They will transfer her to a rehabilitation center in the next couple of days. It will be months before we know how far back she will come."

"I'm terribly sorry," I said taking her hand. "I know you had hoped for better than this."

She nodded her head and absently patted my hand, "You're kind to say so. I have to believe this is just a set back and she'll get well. Matt Alexander came to see her today. She actually smiled."

Mrs. Watson sounded so wistful it was hard not to believe in a full recovery.

We walked back to Michelle's room, "These two detectives need to ask you some questions," her mother told her taking her hand.

Michelle nodded her head to indicate yes.

"My name is Macy McVannel," I told her. "I understand you date Matt Alexander."

Again she nodded yes.

"Did you get a photo e-mailed to you?" I asked.

Her eyes betrayed her horror because we knew and she nodded yes.

"It's okay, you are not the first person this has happened to, but we are working to make sure you are the last," I assured her.

Tom stood silently behind me saying nothing.

"Do you know who sent the photo?" I probed.

As vigorously as she could she nodded yes and tried to speak, "Ch..ch..chel," was all she could get out.

"Chelsie?" I prompted.

Tears ran down her cheeks as she nodded yes.

"Thank you, Michelle, we won't take any more of your time," I told her and we left.

"Are you okay?" I asked Tom as we entered the elevator.

"I couldn't have asked her anything if I'd wanted to," he replied. "I kept seeing Mimi in her place."

"Tom, this is not going to happen to your daughter," I assured him. "We are taking care of the problem and we are going to talk to all the kids in the high school about what will happen if the bullying keeps up." *I wasn't sure we'd be able to do it, but I was going to try and make it happen.*

He smiled, "Thanks, Macy. I guess I just need to separate myself from this case a bit."

"Think nothing of it," I told him. "Consider it part of my job."

We walked to the car in companionable silence and rode back to the police station. I settled in at my desk to write up all we had learned today. Tom headed once again for coffee; *I'd never understand how he could drink the stuff.*

My phone rang and I glanced at the clock as I reached for it thinking: *too late for lunch today.*

"McVannel," I said reaching into my desk for the Snickers bar I kept for just such emergencies.

"Macy, it's Sarah. I have your writing sample."

"Give me a minute to grab Tom and we'll be right over," I replied. I hung up the phone, unwrapped the candy bar, and headed to the break room. "Got the writing sample," I said with my mouthful. Although it came out a bit garbled Tom understood.

"Call the lab first, I want to know if we have her prints on any of those photos," he said.

I returned to my desk, grabbed the phone, and punched the number for the lab.

"Lab, this is Joe."

"McVannel, do you have any prints?" I asked.

"Prints of all kinds. The only match is to one Chelsie Patton."

"Joe, I love you," I shrieked into the phone. "I'm on my way down." I hung up the phone before he could respond.

Tom looked at me oddly as I raced out of the office and to the stairs. He was still standing there when I raced back a few minutes later.

"We've got her!" I yelled. "Let's roll." I grabbed my purse and we headed back to the car.

Once in the car I told him, "Chelsie's fingerprints were on five of the photos. She's been at this for at least two years."

I HAD PULLED myself together by the time we reached Sarah Stephen's office. Marge took one look at us and said, "Go right in she's expecting you."

Tom and I entered Sarah's office grinning.

"Okay, what do you know I don't?" she asked.

We took seats in front of her desk. Tom handed her Mary Golden's diary and I handed her the lab report.

I looked at her smugly and said, "We have a real case against Chelsie Patton."

She looked between the two of us and at the material on her desk, leaned back, and said, "Fill me in."

Tom started, "I just handed you the diary of Mary Golden. She was a girl who dated Matt Alexander a couple years ago. In it she chronicles everything Chelsie and her friends did to her leading to her suicide."

Before Sarah could respond, "I handed you a lab report showing Chelsie Patton's prints were on five of the photos sent to Tansy Taylor also a girl who liked Matt Alexander. Tansy attempted suicide and is now in a private hospital for the mentally impaired."

I waited a moment then handed Sarah a photo in plastic, "Check the writing on the back. Does it look like the sample you just took from Chelsie?"

Sarah reached for the photo, read the sentence on the back, and held the one she had on her desk next to it. "To my untrained eye, they look the same."

"Yesssss," I hissed.

"Slow down, Macy, I need to get a handwriting expert in for verification," she said. Then she turned the photo over to look at it. "Is this Tansy Taylor?"

Tom answered, "It's her head, someone else's body."

"Wow, this girl is good," Sarah said with admiration.

"Good at ruining others," I retorted with disgust.

"In good time, Macy," Sarah said looking up. "I need to read this diary and then I need to talk to you about the other students involved in this mess."

"Most of them are probably victims who bowed to Chelsie," Tom said.

"Have you made any progress on the Ellie Wexford issue?" I asked.

"Slow down you two," Sarah threw up her hands. "I have been very busy. As to Ellie Wexford, her charges can be turned into probation until she is twenty-one, graduated from college, and gainfully employed. What I don't have at this time is a place for her to live. I'm open for suggestions."

I answered first, "We're working on it. I think there might be a place we could send her."

Tom glanced at me curious to know what I was thinking.

I just shook my head, "Let me make a call and I'll have an answer by morning."

Sarah agreed and we moved on, "Are there others who should get probation?"

"Most of the kids who were dragged into this, were victims of Chelsie," I said. "How many can we put on probation?"

"I can do probation for Abby Stark and Katelyn Walker, however Dustin Bell is being charged with statutory rape," she answered.

"Not to mention burglary," I added.

"He's going to do some time, I just don't know what to recommend."

"And our friend, Chelsie Patton?" I asked.

"She's been reckless and her behavior has led to two attempted suicides and one death by suicide," Sarah said thoughtfully. "She's also been indicted on trafficking in pornography of a minor. She's going to do some jail time."

I was satisfied with the answer. Tom said nothing.

"I'll go to work on trial preparation and sentence recommendations for those we feel were victims," she said as if thinking aloud. "Macy, I need to hear from you tomorrow so we can get Ellie Wexford settled."

I nodded and stood. We were done except for writing up the reports and testifying at trial. I stood glad this one was almost done.

CHAPTER
TWENTY-TWO

Tom and I sat at our desks filling out reports on everyone involved in this case. I got up needing a break and walked to the conference room to look at the board before we took it down. Something was niggling at me almost as though I had missed something.

I sat and looked at the photos. *Michelle Watson, Tansy Taylor, and Mary Golden all attempted suicide after being bullied. Matt Alexander would be haunted by this for years to come. Abby Stark sucked in because she threatened Chelsie's self-proclaimed Queen Bee position. Katelyn Walker, who prostituted herself to keep photos of herself from surfacing at the school, Ellie Wexford a victim of child pornography who used her camera to take pornographic photos. Ellie was the issue. We had not come up with a placement for her. Without one she, too would end up doing jail time. We hadn't checked on Mr. Blackburn. Was he a victim, too.* I was so lost in thought I did not hear Tom enter.

"Macy," he said quietly, "Have you found some people to take Ellie in?"

I came out of my reverie and looked at him, "Yes, Mr. and Mrs. Taylor."

"What are you crazy," he almost shouted.

I put my hand on his arm, "Calm down. I've talked to them. They need a reason to keep on. Tansy lives in the hospital and they visit her once a week, but she no longer knows who they are. They need someone who will recognize them and understand they are willing to open their home to them. Besides, they have agreed."

"Do you plan to call Sarah?" he asked still trying to absorb what I was telling him.

"I've already called her. She's going to see them in the morning," I told him. "I think we need to go see Ellie and let her know."

"What if she is against it?" he asked wondering how she would react. "She's been on her own for over two years."

"You and I will be responsible for checking up on her," I told him. "We will see she stays in school, we'll be there when she graduates, we'll even help her choose a college if she asks."

He pondered this for a minute. He liked Ellie and knew she had been handed a raw deal in life. Maybe this is what she needed. Before I knew it, he was smiling. "Sounds like you've got this all planned."

"Just in time to go home for dinner," I said smiling. "Oh no! I have to get home for dinner with Eli." I stood and began taking down the photos from the board. Tom joined me and we were finished in no time.

He placed the photos in our completed file. As I reached for my purse, I said, "We can talk to her in the morning. I also want to talk to the superintendent at the school. I think we need to talk to the students before all this is in the paper and there is speculation."

"I'm in," he told me. "Your idea of talking to the kids is a good one," he continued. "They need to know what to do if they are being bullied. The teachers need to be more aware."

"Maybe we can pass out our cards so the kids can reach us," I suggested.

"We're going to be a presence," Tom assured me.

"I hate to rain on your parade," I started. "But we need to follow-up on the computer teacher, Mr. Blackburn. I have a sneaking suspicion he is a victim, too."

"It will wait until, morning," Tom assured me.

Walking companionably, we left the building headed to our respective homes and yes, families.

MY HOUSE HAD an empty feel when I walked in. I had not realized the difference it made knowing Eli would be waiting for me. It was as if the life had been sucked out of the house. I slowly went up the stairs, did my after work stint in the work-out room and showered.

I piled my hair up on my head letting the curls fall where they would, put on my favorite perfume and a pale aqua dress. I added a pair of low heels and took stock of myself in the full-length mirror in my room.

Not bad, even if it was just me. So why did I feel like a teen getting ready for her first date? This was Eli for heaven's sake. I shook myself before I could start with the self-doubts.

Making my way downstairs, I put on the porch light and waited for Eli to arrive. I found myself pacing between the living room and dining room. *Telling myself this was silly I made myself sit at the table. When that didn't work, I started pacing again.* I jumped when Eli rang the doorbell.

I opened the door and he stood there looking as handsome as he had the first night in the bunkhouse. Dark hair falling over one eyebrow, blue eyes sparkling as though they held a secret, he looked like something from every young girl's dream.

Saying nothing, he folded me into his arms and kissed me. When he stopped he whispered, "You look sensational."

Smiling I told him, "You don't look half-bad yourself."

"Are you ready?" he asked.

"Lead the way," I told him. We locked the door and went to his car. I was not surprised to see the he was driving a sports car in a beautiful shade of blue. "Oh, my we are going in style," I chuckled.

"I borrowed it from my brother," he said. "I didn't think you'd want to go anyplace in my beat up old truck."

I got in rolling my eyes. *Thinking, I'd go anywhere with you in anything.*

Eli closed my door then walked around the car to get in. As we backed out of the driveway he said, "I hope you'll like the surprise."

"What surprise?" I asked suddenly on alert.

"The location for our dinner," he said. "Relax, Macy, it's just us."

I let out the breath I had been holding. I had been sure he had planned something and I did not want people around tonight. I wanted to just be with Eli. He took my hand and we were off.

We drove for miles, with Eli putting in a jazz CD. The music was soothing and I found myself relaxing. I gasped when we pulled into the Log Cabin Inn. They were famous for their privacy and catered to the rich and famous. I glanced at Eli who was smiling. He pulled up in front and a doorman came down to open my door another opened Eli's door and took the keys. Valet parking, doormen, we were going to the Ritz.

The maitre'd led us to a private room where the table was elegantly set with fine china and crystal. Candles were lit on the table and around the room. The room was filled with yellow roses and lily of the valley. As I took it in, I saw the French doors opened onto a private patio.

I looked at Eli, his eyes were shining. He had done all this for me, my favorite flowers and candlelight. The maitre'd opened a bottle of champagne which had been chilling and poured us each a glass. He handed them to us and discreetly left the room.

"This is fabulous, Eli," I gushed.

He nodded sipping his champagne before saying, "I'm glad you like it."

"To think I was worried," I told him. "Maybe I should have dressed up a bit more." Sipping the champagne I looked around again.

"Would you care to walk the gardens?" he asked.

I nodded and took the arm he offered. *I knew I'd wake up soon. I felt like a princess in a fairytale. No one had gone to this length for me before.*

We strolled the gardens, sipping our champagne, not talking. The autumn flowers were beautiful in the soft light. I heard occasional laughter and glasses tinkling, but we saw no one. As we approached the patio again, Eli put our glasses on a table and turned to me, "Would you care to dance?

"I'd love to," I told him. "But are you sure it's okay?"

"Doctor gave me the all clear as long as I stay away from the jitterbug," he answered taking me in his arms I heard the faint sound of violins. A beautiful waltz sounded from nearby. Although I looked, I could not see the musicians. Eli masterfully led me around the patio. I knew I could dance like this all night.

After another song had played, Eli stopped taking my hands and led me into the room where our salads had been set.

I still had the feeling of being in a fairytale. He held my chair for me and then joined me at the table.

"Are you happy?" he asked.

"Speechless," I breathed.

We ate our salads and I was not aware when the plates were removed. Eli was my whole focus. Neither of us talked much. A cup of clam chowder appeared in front of me, I ate almost on auto pilot.

Dinner was a grilled chicken breast served on angel hair pasta with a light cheese and garlic sauce. It was delicious.

"I have no idea where you found this place," I said. "But I truly am glad you did. Everything is wonderful."

Eli smiled, "I'm glad you like it. The owner is a family friend and he let me into the kitchen to make our dinner."

"You made all this," I was stunned.

"I told you I studied to be a chef," he was smiling. "I wanted to really show off."

"You should open a restaurant," I teased. "This is fabulous."

"I admit to sneaking into your cook books to see which recipes you used the most," he told me unabashedly. "I took those recipes and created my version for dinner."

Smiling I reached for his hand, "This is amazing. I really do think you should open a restaurant."

"And miss the action of desk work at the police station," he pretended to be appalled.

We laughed and I made a toast to his wonderful dinner. After we were done, we walked the garden again.

"I suppose you wouldn't believe me if I told you I own a restaurant," Eli said as we walked.

"You do?" I raised my eyebrows at him.

"Yes," he said seriously. "I own this one."

I stopped walking to look at him. *Was he pulling my leg? Why hadn't he told me this before?* I was confused.

"Please say something," he pleaded.

"I'm speechless," I breathed. "Why didn't you ever tell me this?"

He took both of my hands, "I wanted you to love me for the person I am. Too many women like me for the money I have."

Stunned I could only stare at him. "You thought I was shallow? I was a gold digger? Yet, you told me you loved me?" I was incredulous.

"I do love you," he said. "I never thought you were shallow."

"But you just said," I began, pulling my hands from his and starting back toward the patio.

Eli let me go, knowing I needed to walk off my confusion and anger. I was back inside when he finally came through the door. "How could you?" I demanded.

"I knew you had your own demons to deal with, I didn't want to force mine on you, too," he responded. "I was wrong. I should have told you."

"We have a lot to learn about each other," I said. "Maybe we should call it a day."

"Please not before dessert," he said smiling.

I glanced at the table seeing heart shaped cakes sitting at each of our places. Never one to waste food I sat and told him, "Okay, dessert then home."

We ate our desserts in silence. It was a chocolate cake with a raspberry filling and pink frosting. I believed this was almost heaven and found myself thawing toward Eli. After all, he had made this wonderful dinner for me.

Driving home I slid my hand in his, "Are there any other secrets I should know?"

"No," he said keeping his eyes on the road. "I believe you know all of them now."

"Good," I said, "because I'm not fond of surprises. Please don't do things designed to make me feel foolish. I manage to get into trouble on my own. I still cannot believe I would have cared if you owned a restaurant or were wealthy." I paused then found myself giggling.

"What's so funny?" he asked glancing at me.

"We are," I continued to giggle. "I think we've had our first fight. But I don't know who won."

He smiled, "We both did. We learned to be open with each other."

At my house, he walked me to the door and kissed me a passionate good-night. I let myself in and locked the door, watching as he drove away. Then I turned out the porch light and went upstairs to bed.

Remembering our evening, I walked to my room dropping my clothing where they fell. As I tumbled into bed, I drifted to sleep dreaming of being held in Eli's arms.

CHAPTER TWENTY-THREE

Saturday

I awoke slowly stretching my arms and legs, sunlight coming through the curtains. I leaped out of bed, threw on a pair of sweats, and started down the stairs. The phone rang bringing me out of my own thoughts. "McVannel," I said picking it up.

"Macy, aren't we going to talk to Ellie?" Tom asked.

"What, what time is it?" I said glancing at the clock on the stove. I groaned.

"I'll pick you up in ten minutes," Tom snapped.

"Okay," I said hanging up the phone before he could say more. I ran up the stairs and changed into dress pants, a blouse, and jacket. I was downstairs finishing a cup of tea and grabbing an apple as Tom pulled in. I raced to the car.

"I'm sorry I overslept," I said as I buckled my seat belt.

"Must have been some dinner," was all he said. I bit into my apple and said nothing.

"Sorry, I didn't mean to pry," Tom said quickly. "I just think Eli is good for you."

We drove to Last Chance Center. Tom had called yesterday and they were expecting us. We signed in and surrendered our weapons. A different clerk led us to the library. Today, Ellie was reading when we entered.

"So are you going to spring me or am I stuck here for life?" she asked with false bravado.

"We have a proposition for you," Tom said.

"I'm listening," she said.

Tom and I sat on a sofa across from her, "We can get your charges reduced to probation," I began.

"What's the catch?" she asked knowingly.

"We have arranged for you to live with a couple whose daughter was a victim of Chelsie Patton," I said. "They have agreed to take you into their home."

"Like I said, what's the catch?" she repeated.

I told her, "There are several conditions."

"And if I'm not interested?" she knew she was pushing.

"We arrange for you to do jail time until you are twenty-one," was Tom's blunt statement.

She blanched knowing she had pushed too far, "Okay, let's hear the conditions."

"First, Tom and I are your probation officers. Which means we will be checking weekly to see you are following the plan we've set up," I told her. "You will attend school every day you are not physically ill. If you are ill, you will be seen by a doctor. You will do chores assigned to you by Mr. and Mrs. Taylor. There will be no back talk. Tom and I will be at your graduation and we expect you to find a college to attend in the fall. You should plan to work during the summer. While you are at college, we will be checking in on you weekly, either by phone or visits. No, we won't call ahead. When you have graduated from college and are gainfully employed, we will release you from probation. Do you have any questions?"

"Tell me about Mr. and Mrs. Taylor," she said almost shyly.

"Their daughter Tansy was dating Matt Alexander a couple of years ago. Chelsie knew she was a dancer and took photos of strippers and photoshopped Tansy's head onto them. Tansy attempted suicide and instead of dying ended up with fried brain cells. The Taylors are lost. They need a young person to bring life into their lives. They might even ask you to visit Tansy with them," Tom told her.

"Can I photograph Tansy now?" Ellie asked. "I think someone should document the bad things Chelsie has done."

"It's something you will have to discuss with the Taylors," I told her.

"Ellie, I'd like to ask you to do something else," I said.

"Fire, what is it?" she replied.

"We are going to be talking to the students at Rivers Edge High about bullying. Will you speak up, too?" I asked.

"Sure, I never liked taking the photos for Chelsie. Will I still be going there?"

"No," I answered. "You'll be attending school in the district where the Taylor's live."

"Okay, but…" she hesitated. Tom and I waited expecting a protest. "Could we speak at my new school, too?"

We looked at each other, "We'll look into the possibility," Tom told her.

"Will I get a dark room?" she wanted to know.

"I had a long talk with Mr. Taylor. He has an unused shed on his property and thinks the two of you could move your things to it, with the condition he and his wife can enter whenever you're not developing film," Tom said. "Secretly I think he wants to learn how you do it." He winked at Ellie.

She ignored the wink saying, "Way cool. I'll do everything you ask."

"We should be able to spring you on Monday morning, for your first meeting with the Taylors and to get you enrolled in the new school," I told her.

Her smile said it all. We left her reading her book.

In the car, Tom looked at me and said, "I'm calling Shannon to let her know we'll be there for lunch. Do you want to call Eli?"

Smiling I grabbed my cell and made the call. I knew as soon as Tom called Shannon she would call JJ and Sally Mae. We would be getting ready for the baptism tomorrow.

CHAPTER TWENTY-FOUR

Sunday

I was up well before my alarm. I had done my workout and showered. Breakfast was eaten and the dishes were done. Now I had to get ready for one of the biggest days of my life. Mimi was being baptized and JJ, Sally Mae, Eli, and I were her godparents. The enormity of the job seemed to hit me all of the sudden. *What had I gotten into?* Heading up the stairs to get ready I thought about what it meant to be a godmother. *It meant remembering birthdays, holidays, special events, and keeping Mimi believing what her parents said and did was for her own good. What was I thinking to agree? It was almost like raising a child of my own.* I smiled and thought about taking Eli to meet my family afterward.

My brother, Mitchell is everything I am not, tall, brown eyed, and what I think of as a man's man. He likes hunting, fishing, and sporting events. His family is everything to him. He sets goals and achieves them. He wanted to be an attorney and is a successful one. When he met Elizabeth, his Bitsy, he did everything in his power to make her fall in love with him. They worked at making marriage work. I wondered if I could.

I finished dressing in a green print skirt with a matching sweater. I found a necklace to put on. I pulled the sides of my hair back into a clip and let the curls fall, as they were want to do anyway.

Eli pulled in as I was coming down the stairs. I reached the front door as he was about to knock.

"Are you ready?" he asked.

"I think so, let me grab my purse," I answered.

He waited as I grabbed my purse. We walked to the car hand-in-hand. It felt right.

"Are you nervous?" I asked as he drove to the church.

"No, should I be?" he smiled at me as though giving me confidence.

I smiled back, "Probably not. It just seems to be a lot to take on."

"You'll do fine and Mimi will be a great godchild," he assured me. "I was worried you were thinking about your family."

"My family?" I queried.

"I am meeting them today," he reminded me.

"Oh," I said quietly. "I can only worry about one thing at a time, Mimi's baptism comes first," I chuckled as I said it.

"That's my girl," Eli said squeezing my hand.

JJ and Sally Mae were waiting outside the church for us. JJ looked like he had been pacing.

"It's a good thing you two arrived," Sally Mae started in. "You'd think it was a wedding and JJ was the nervous groom. He's been pacing a hole in the sidewalk." She laughed.

JJ stopped pacing long enough to give me a quick hug and shake hands with Eli. "What if I screw this up?" he asked.

"There's nothing to screw up," Eli assured him, "when the minister asks, just say 'yes'."

"Easy for you to say," JJ countered.

"Quit worrying and let's go inside," Sally Mae said. She sounded like a mother hen collecting her chicks. JJ and Sally Mae preceded us up the stairs. We joined Ida, Angela Waxman, Tom, Shannon, and the kids then made our way down the aisle toward the front of the church.

The ceremony was beautiful. No one 'screwed up' as JJ so succinctly phrased it. Mimi was wonderful during the whole thing and the boys were intrigued.

Afterward, Eli and I begged off lunch and headed for my brother's. It was a good two hour drive.

"My brother, Mitch is older than I am and tends to be protective," I told Eli. "Don't let him put you off."

He took my hand and said, "I think I can handle your brother."

I found myself relaxing and looking forward to the afternoon with my family and Eli.

"So, this is where you grew up," Eli said looking around as we pulled into the old neighborhood.

"Pretty much," I answered. "We lived a couple blocks over as kids. Mitch wanted to be near Mom and Dad."

"Our families are what keep us going," Eli said not really looking for a reply.

He parked across the street from my brother's and we locked the car and walked toward the backyard.

I was immediately surrounded by nieces and nephews losing Eli's hand in the mix. Laughter surrounded us as I was dragged off to see other family members. I stiffened when I turned and saw Mitch approaching Eli. I could not hear what they were saying but, both of them were smiling and Mitch showed Eli where to find food and beverages. I was again wrapped in the arms of the younger children as they begged to be first to tell their latest escapades.

Eli was pretty scarce most of the afternoon. I worried he would get bored. I found him under a tree with my Aunt Lois. He smiled looking up at me.

"Your Aunt Lois has been telling me what a handful you were as a child," he chuckled.

"Macy, if you know what's good for you," Aunt Lois started, "you'll keep this young man around." She gave me the look that said, 'Time you settled down.'

I hugged Aunt Lois and said, "I'll see what I can do." I rolled my eyes at Eli. I should have known he would charm them all.

We said our good-byes as others were leaving and headed for home. *Part of me wished Eli was coming to my home. Part of me knew it would be a mistake.* The ride was uneventful and I fell asleep half-way. Waking only as I felt the car slow to turn into my driveway.

"Glad you are awake," Eli said getting out of the car.

"I didn't sleep well last night," I admitted. "I'm sorry I fell asleep."

He smiled, "It's okay. I love watching you sleep."

"Coming in?" I asked as we started up the walk.

"Only for a minute," he said.

"No coffee or anything?"

He winked and said, "I'll think about the anything."

As soon as the front door closed, Eli wrapped me in his arms and kissed me lifting me off the floor. I clung to him as my world spun out of control.

He set me gently on the floor and said, "I'll call you sometime tomorrow."

"You're leaving?" I asked breathlessly.

"I told you I'd think about the anything. I thought about it and kissing you will just lead us to another dilemma," he told me. "I want to give you space, but I never want you to forget I love you." He turned and let himself out the door.

Well, I wasn't going to forget that kiss anytime soon. As the thought crossed my mind I growled, then headed up the stairs to have another workout.

CHAPTER TWENTY-FIVE

Monday

The early bird is supposed to catch the worm, so I was at the station an hour before shift started. I put in a search for Jeremy Blackstone. He was possibly one more person Chelsie had victimized. Sarah Stephens planned to call Tom and me to testify today. We were probably all she would have time for after Mrs. Watson was questioned. We were due in court at ten and I wanted to get there early. I was sure the local paper would be there covering this, but I was not sure if the television station had picked it up. If they had, things could be a zoo.

By the time Tom arrived I had cleaned the coffee pot and put on a fresh pot to brew. He came into the break room looking for me.

"The coffee smells really good," he commented picking up his cup. "How long have you been here and what did you do to this room?"

"I was an hour early and nervous energy happened to this room," I told him.

Laughing he poured himself a cup of coffee. He took a sip and said, "This is really good. You sure it came from this pot?"

"It needed a good cleaning is all," I chuckled.

"When do you want to go to the courthouse?"

"No small talk about yesterday?" I questioned.

Shrugging he replied, "Only if you want to talk."

Pausing for a moment before answering, "Nope," was my reply as I left the room.

Tom finished his coffee and joined me in the squad room. "Do you want to walk or drive to the courthouse?"

I looked up and said, "Let's walk; I seem to have too much energy this morning." I grabbed my purse where I had already put my case notes and stood.

Reaching for his case notes, Tom followed behind me.

"Macy," Tom said as we walked out of the building, "Shannon super cleans when something is bothering her or when she is pregnant. You haven't known Eli long enough for me to worry you're expecting, so tell me what it is."

I looked at him long and hard before answering, "Did you know Eli owns the Log Cabin Inn?"

"Holy cow! No way!" Tom exclaimed as he stopped walking to face me.

"He told me Friday night when he took me to dinner there," I confessed. "It bugs me he felt he had to hide it from me."

"You met him in his capacity as a police officer," Tom told me calmly. "Maybe he was unsure of how you would feel about him being an entrepreneur."

I shrugged and started walking again. Tom matched my stride and said nothing. Finally I blurted out, "I don't care what he does for a living. I care about *him.*"

"Well, you're making progress," Tom chuckled. "You have admitted you care."

I growled and kept walking. Tom said nothing more until we reached the courthouse. "You up for this?" he asked.

Looking him squarely in the eye I replied, "More ready than you can imagine. I want this girl taken down."

We quietly entered the courtroom to wait for the proceedings to begin.

DUSTIN BELL'S CASE was up first on the docket. Bart Miller was seated at the defense table waiting for his client to be brought in. Dustin had been held in custody since being arrested. I was curious to see how he would appear as the trial got underway.

We did not have long to wait. Dustin was led in and uncuffed when they reached the defense table. I was surprised to see him in prison orange. The bailiff entered and said, "All rise for the Honorable Judge Elizabeth Allen.

The judge entered from her chambers, as she seated herself the bailiff told us to be seated. Then he called the first case, "State of Michigan vs Dustin Bell one count of criminal sexual conduct with a minor, one count of trafficking in pornography of a minor."

The judge looked out at the courtroom asking, "Is the prosecution ready?"

Sarah Stephens stood and replied, "Yes, your Honor.

"Defense are you ready to proceed?" the judge asked.

"We are your Honor," Miller replied as he stood.

"It has come to my attention a plea agreement has been reached," the judge began.

Sarah answered, "It has, your Honor."

Bart Miller nodded in the affirmative.

"I have read the agreement and am satisfied this is in the best interests of everyone involved. Young man," she said looking at Dustin, "you are being given a chance to clean up your act. Had this gone to trial you would have been facing a minimum of fifteen years in jail. Do you understand what you are agreeing to?"

Dustin stood and replied, "Yes, your Honor, I do."

"Very well, you will be sentenced to a minimum of ten years in prison with time off for good behavior. You could be paroled in half the time. Providing you keep your nose clean," she said with no emotion.

"Thank you, your Honor," Dustin surprised everyone by saying anything.

There might be hope for this one yet. Chelsie had done him an injustice by promising she would provide him with a virgin. I was pleased with the way this had turned out, although prison would not be kind to Dustin.

The judge brought down her gavel indicating this case was closed. Chelsie Patton was not due on the docket until after lunch.

"This court will be in recess until one o'clock," the judge said.

As she finished the bailiff once again said, "All rise." We rose as the judge left the bench.

THERE WOULD BE for us grand jury testimony after lunch. We were hoping to get it through in one day. It did not look like it was going to happen. Sarah caught up with us in the hallway.

"The bad news is Chelsie Patton is planning to take the stand in her own defense," Sarah began, "The good news is her attorney cannot ask questions."

I smiled, "Is this going to impact us?"

"Not really," she answered. "I don't have to let the attorney into the grand jury room, but I will."

Tom grinned, "Going to give him a taste of what he's up against?"

"Sure, am," she replied. "But I don't see this as a slam dunk. The girl was smart until the computer photo came out. She should have quit while she was ahead."

"It's the problem with kids who think they are smarter than everyone else," I told her. While my experience with kids was limited to my nieces and nephews, I could see when they were trying to push the parental envelope. "Are you joining us at the deli for lunch?"

Sarah shook her head. "As much as I'd love to, I have other cases to prepare. Maybe next time," she said walking toward the elevators.

As Tom and I walked to the deli we talked about how we thought the grand jury would go. "I'm sure they'll indict for something," Tom said, "I don't see what Sarah sees as an obstacle."

"We made sure she has all her ducks in a row," I answered. "But you never know what a grand jury thinks."

Finding an empty booth in the back we took it. The waitress brought cups and a pot of coffee. Tom accepted the coffee, I asked for hot tea. We pretended to study the menus while the waitress went to get my tea. When she returned I ordered a chicken salad sandwich and Tom ordered a bowl of loaded chili.

"Tell me more about Eli and the Log Cabin Inn," he prompted.

"We went Friday night for dinner," I began, "As we were walking through the private garden after dinner he told me he owned it. I don't know what he was expecting, but I behaved badly."

"I imagine it was a bit of a shock," Tom acquiesced.

"Shock! I was angry," I told him. "Mad because he thought I was a gold digger. I don't know just frustrated." I was steamed just thinking about it.

"There is no way Eli thinks you're a gold digger," Tom assured me. "The man is head-over-heels in love with you. I think you made a big step today admitting you care about him."

I looked at Tom long and hard, "I don't just care about him. I'm in love with him, but I can't bring myself to tell him." It was a hard admission for me to make.

The waitress brought our food and no one said anything for a few minutes while we ate.

Conversation returned to the case at hand, "I'm up first in the grand jury," Tom commented.

"You okay?" I asked.

"As okay as I'm ever going to be," he answered shaking his head as if to clear cobwebs. "I hate cases where kids are involved. It makes me uncomfortable."

"It makes us all uncomfortable and this case is as bad as it gets," I told him. "We don't usually get called to investigate attempted suicides. I never suspected bullying had reached this level."

Tom nodded in agreement. "Shannon and I have been grilling the boys since this started. I think they believe we've lost it."

I chuckled, "It does make you question what you've taught your kids, doesn't it?"

"Not just what we've taught them, but whether or not they have been the victims of bullying is what's most frightening," he said smiling.

We finished up and paid our bill. Heading back to the courthouse we proceeded to the hallway outside the grand jury room. Procedure is each person comes in individually, gives their testimony, and answers anything unclear to grand jury members. It is not like a trial where there is no interaction with the jury. Grand jury members are allowed to ask questions for clarification. No one cross-examines you. The grand jury is looking at the facts presented to see if there is enough evidence to warrant a jury trial. While it is a tedious process at times, it is also a safe guard to protect against civil rights violations.

Tom was called first. His testimony took thirty minutes. I was up next. My testimony took closer to forty-five minutes. Next, would come the testimony of those who would be witnesses against Chelsie. First up was Dustin Bell, because he was still in the building after his own hearing. Ellie Wexford would be called as well as Abby Stark, Katelyn Walker, and Matt Alexander. I was pretty sure there would be others. It would take the rest of the afternoon and possibly into tomorrow morning for everyone to testify. Chelsie even had the option to attend; although it seemed unlikely her attorney would notify the court of their intent to be present.

When I was finished, Tom and I walked back to the station. "How do you read the jury?" Tom asked.

"I don't try to read juries," I told him. "I get a feeling sometimes on how I think they'll go, but I'm not worried about this one. They are going to be appalled and will make this go to trial for something."

Tom shrugged, "I hope so."

Something was bugging him again, his body was tense. "So, what has you trying to second guess the jury?"

Looking at me he said, "Ellie has probation until she's twenty-one. We even found her a decent home. Dustin is heading for jail. Katelyn is going to be tried as a child and will probably get probation. Abby has turned on Chelsie and will probably get probation. Chelsie on the other hand, is looking at serious jail time. Is it fair?"

"You're not serious?" I questioned. "Spoiled rich kid who thinks laws are for someone else and doesn't care who she hurts. Are you nuts?"

"Not when you put it in those terms," he agreed.

"It's the only way to put it," I answered hotly. "She has a blatant disregard for the welfare of others. She's a sociopath. By the time she graduated, I suspect hiring hit men would not be beneath her."

"You are probably right. It's just they are kids," Tom lamented.

"The kind of kids who make you hate all teenagers," I scoffed.

BACK IN THE squad room there calls to answer, reports to finish, and general grunt work which had been put off and needed to be done. I dug right in. Tom was still brooding and went to get himself a cup of coffee.

The background check on Jeremy Blackburn had come in. I read through it and made a call to set up an interview with him.

The call came about an hour later and Tom took it. I could only hear his side of the conversation. "Maxwell."

"So, we move on the issues of prostitution and pornography with blatant disregard for others. Okay, sure we'll be there." He hung up the phone.

He looked at me and said, "The grand jury found sufficient grounds to recommend charges of prostitution and pornography, with a blatant disregard for others. They are doing jury selection now. We are expected in court tomorrow at nine."

"We need to interview Jeremy Blackburn, he'll be waiting for us in an hour," I told Tom.

"Let's roll."

We left together with Tom driving. Blackburn was going to meet us at his home about thirty-five minutes away. When we arrived he was just pulling into his driveway. He waited for us then led the way to his front door.

"Please come in and have a seat," he said graciously. "Can I get either of you something to drink?"

"No, thank you," Tom told him. We took seats on his sofa and Tom pulled out the notebook.

Jeremy Blackburn was in his late twenties a bit on the heavy side, with sandy hair and a full beard. He sat in a chair and said, "Ask me anything you'd like."

"It is my understanding you blocked a website at Rivers Edge High School last year," I started.

He shook his head, "You must mean the supposed porn site all the kids were looking at."

"Yes, what can you tell us about it?"

"To the best of my understanding it was started as a cruel joke," he began. "The young lady in question left school. I don't know what happened to her."

"She is being home-schooled. How did you happen to leave?"

"I went seeking the source of the website and traced it to another student," he said sadly. "My mistake was confronting the student."

He had my full attention. "May I ask which student and why it was a mistake?"

"The student was Chelsie Patton. I traced the IP-Internet Provider-address back to her computer. When I confronted her, she became belligerent and insulting. Two days later I found myself in the principal's office with a union rep and a photo of me in a compromising position with another student," he was embarrassed. "I explained the photo had been doctored, but my career at Rivers Edge High was over. They gave me a glowing recommendation and gave me a severance to keep me from saying anything."

"Would you be willing to testify to this in court?" I asked.

"Only if I have to," he said. "But why is it an issue now?"

"Because Chelsie has been arrested and is awaiting trial on several charges of bullying," I told him. "One girl has died and two others have attempted suicide, because of the things she's done."

He actually smiled, "Under those circumstances, you can have my testimony. I don't like what she does to people."

Tom stood. "Thank you for your time Mr. Blackburn. If your testimony is needed you will hear from the Assistant District Attorney."

Blackburn shook hands with both of us; you could almost feel the gratitude he had. We left heading back for the station.

Tom spoke first, "I wondered about this when you wanted to check into him. The girl is evil."

"I agree.

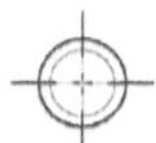

WE RETURNED TO work on the report of this interview. I wanted to give it to Sarah tomorrow.

After an hour I said, "I guess I should finish up here and head home."

Less than ten minutes later, I had things done and was on my way out the door. Tom was right behind me.

CHAPTER TWENTY-SIX

Again the emptiness of my house when enveloped me when I entered. Eli moving back to his place had sucked the warmth right out of my home. It also made me admit I enjoyed having him here. Making my way to the fridge I decided to find something for dinner.

I chuckled inside the door hanging down was a note. *Don't make plans for dinner it's being delivered around six.*

Not having dinner to worry about I decided I would do another work out. I did my rotations, showered, and had my new sweats on when Eli arrived with dinner. There was spinach salad, baked chicken breasts, green beans, and dessert. I quickly set the table and found a chilled bottle of white wine. Eli produced some rolls and butter from the bags and we sat down to eat.

We passed idle chit-chat about our day. When dinner was over Eli helped clean up. "You seem a bit subdued," he said.

"I'm just distracted," I told him. "Tom is starting to feel sorry for Chelsie Patton because her sentence will most likely be the longest." I shrugged.

Eli came to me, taking me in his arms. "This has been a tough one hasn't it?"

I nodded in agreement. "I want it over. I want this girl to get what is coming to her."

"How about we watch a movie?" he suggested, "something funny to take your mind off the case."

I agreed and we perused my movies to find something silly and curled up on the sofa together. I could feel myself relaxing as the movie started and we laughed all the way through it. Eli picked a second movie; by then I did not care he went for an action movie. I curled into him and fell asleep.

It was oblivion for me until Eli kissed me.

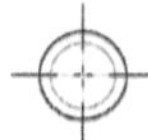

TUESDAY

I awoke still in my sweats and in my bed. There was a note on my nightstand. It said: *I set your alarm so you wouldn't be late. Dinner tonight? I love you. Eli.*

Heading to do my morning workout I found a second note on my treadmill. *Have a great day. Love, Eli*

Smiling I completed my workout and headed to the shower. It was not until I stepped out I noticed the third note. Eli had taken some lipstick I rarely use and drawn a big heart with Eli loves Macy in the center. I found myself smiling as I dressed for the day. Downstairs in the fridge I found yet another note: *Something simple for dinner tonight. Do you object to pizza? Love, Eli.* I also found a breakfast bagel ready to pop in the microwave. I heated it, made a cup of tea, and headed to my car. It was no surprise there was yet another note: *Drive safe. I love you, Eli*

Once at work I settled in to any work which had crossed my desk during the night. Tom was not far behind me; he set a cup of tea on my desk and said, "We need to think about heading to the courthouse. Opening statements are first up today."

"Let me finish my tea and I'll be ready," I said taking a big drink.

We walked the two blocks to the courthouse. Once we passed through the checkpoint we took our seats in the courtroom. As always I was awed by the reverence of the room. Sometimes I wished the walls would tell me their secrets, other times I wished I never had to be in a court room.

People began filtering in; Mr. and Mrs. Patton sat in the row directly behind the defense table. Mrs. Patton looked drawn while Mr. Patton held himself erect as if the whole situation were beneath him. *I no longer wondered where Chelsie found her superior attitude.* A few reporters filled in the back of the court room. I could see sketch books come out. Cameras were not going to be allowed in the court room today.

Barney Bradford sauntered in and seated himself at the defense table. Tom and I shared a look. The Pattons had called in the big guns. Bradford was known to play to the cameras, which explained why there were none today. He was also a well-known criminal defense attorney. Sarah would have her work cut out for her.

Chelsie was brought in and seated at the defense table at the same time Sarah arrived. Her mother attempted to reach out to her but the girl blew her off. I suspected she thought she was invincible with Barney Bradford sitting next to her. No wonder he wanted to go straight to trial. This was going to be interesting.

The bailiff entered and proclaimed, "All rise for the Honorable Judge Elizabeth Allen."

The entire room rose as one. Judge Allen entered and took her seat at the bench. "You may be seated. Bailiff, please bring in the jury."

Jury selection had happened earlier in the week while we finished up the investigation. I watched as the jury came in. Pleased as

I saw a wide variety of people; some were in their twenties, some in their thirties, the rest between forty and sixty. There was also a mix of men and women, Blacks, Hispanics, and whites. In my opinion, they had done a good job.

The bailiff spoke, "The State of Michigan vs Chelsie Patton charged with distribution of pornography of a minor, use of cell phone and internet for purposes of distribution, creating fraudulent websites, and pandering for the purpose of prostitution. Amended charges include: harassment leading to suicide and attempted suicide as well as reckless endangerment."

Chelsie blanched when the prostitution charge was read. I was sure she was going to speak out, but she did not. *I wondered how long she would be able to sit there and hold her spiteful tongue. Just because she was dressed to look demure did not mean she was.*

Judge Allen looked at Sarah, "Is the prosecution ready?"

Sarah stood and responded, "Yes, your Honor."

The judge turned to the defense, "Is the defense ready?"

Bradford stood, "Defense is ready, your Honor." He appeared to bow slightly before sitting back down.

"Proceed with your opening Ms. Stephens," the judge directed.

Sarah stood and walked toward the jury, "Good morning ladies and gentlemen."

"Good morning," they answered in unison.

"Today you are going to hear things bad enough to turn your stomachs. You will however; have to put your emotions aside, listen to testimony, and see the evidence against Chelsie Patton. She is accused of some heinous crimes against her classmates. She has blackmailed friends into doing things they would not normally have had a reason to do. She has bribed others to do her dirty work and caused three young women to attempt suicide to escape her torment. She is heartless. Chelsie Patton thinks everyone should bow to her will and if they don't she finds a way to make their lives miserable.

This is bullying at its worst. Listen carefully to all you will hear so you can make a sound judgment when the time comes."

Sarah paused then returned to her seat at the prosecution table.

"Mr. Bradford," said the judge.

Bradford stood and approached the jury, "Good morning, I want to thank you for giving your time to hear this case. Chelsie Patton is a child of wealth and as one has been spoiled. She is not a monster as the prosecution would have you believe, but a young girl with a misguided impression of how things should be done. She has not physically harmed anyone. She did not threaten the young women who attempted suicide. She is in no way to blame for the actions of others. The prosecution will try to paint my client as a monster; she is nothing more than a teenage girl involved in girl drama. Please listen carefully as the assistant district attorney recommended. See this girl for what she really is; a teen."

With those words he returned to the defense table. *I was in awe of his ability to twist the truth into something as simple as 'girl drama.' This girl is a monster of the worst kind, because most of them do not get caught.*

"Call your first witness, Ms. Stephens."

Standing Sarah said, "The state calls Detective Sgt. McVannel."

I took a deep breath and rose. I walked to the witness stand where I was sworn in by the bailiff. Settling into the chair I faced the jury.

"Please state your name and occupation," Sarah began.

"Macy McVannel, Detective Sergeant with the Rivers Edge Police Department," I stated succinctly.

"How did you come to be involved in this case?"

"I received a call from your office asking me to bring my partner," I responded.

"What did you find once you arrived at my office?"

"A distraught woman was with you," I continued to keep my answers limited to the questions.

"Were you introduced?"

"Yes, the woman was Mrs. Watson."

"What did you learn from Mrs. Watson?"

It was getting easier, "Her daughter attempted suicide."

"Why would you investigate a suicide attempt?"

"It was apparent something outside her family had caused Michelle to try to take her life."

"Why do you say, 'outside her family,'" Sarah continued to press.

"Mrs. Watson knew of a photograph which had been circulated at the high school."

Sarah took something from a file on the prosecution table. "We stipulate this photograph to be state's exhibit one. Is this the photograph?"

The judge looked to the defense table. Bradford nodded, "Defense stipulates to the photograph?"

Sarah handed me the photograph. "Yes, this is the one." I said and handed it back. Sarah walked it to the jury.

As the jury members passed the photograph amongst them, Sarah continued to question me, "What did you learn about the photograph?"

"The defendant, Chelsie Patton sent it from her computer to everyone in the school."

"When confronted with this evidence, what did the defendant do?"

"She refused to speak until her parents arrived, then pretended to be intimidated and gave sarcastic answers to our questions. She was subsequently arrested."

"Did she become more forthcoming after being arrested?"

"No, she continued to be belligerent."

"Thank you, Detective McVannel, no further questions."

The judge looked at the defense and asked, "Cross-examine?"

"We have no questions at this time."

"You may step down, Detective McVannel," the judge said.

I stepped down and walked back to my seat. *I was confused as to why the defense did not question how we came to discover Chelsie had sent the photo.*

Tom was called next and answered some of the same questions I had been asked. Again the defense waived cross-examination at this time. *Puzzling. I wondered what was going on. Was he going to let everyone off as easy? It did not seem like he would.*

The judge called a recess and told us to return at one. She felt additional witnesses would take us into the lunch hour.

Sarah caught up to us as people were filing out of the court-room. "Do you have time to go over something with me?"

"Sure," Tom answered.

We followed her to a conference room. "What's up?" I asked.

"My first witness against Chelsie Patton comes up after lunch," Sarah began making sure the door was locked. "I've offered deals they have all been turned down. This girl believes she is invincible."

"Chelsie thinks because she is a first time offender all she is going to get is probation," I told her.

"Well, she needs someone to counsel her. Probation is not even a consideration," Sarah said hotly.

Tom ever the voice of reason asked, "What is it you want from us?"

"I thought you'd never ask," Sarah smiled as she answered. "I need to know if we can get her mental records."

"Mental records," I asked in shock.

"Evidently she was hospitalized at about eleven or twelve for some kind of breakdown," she explained. "I don't want to be blind-sided if the defense puts it in as an explanation for what she's done."

"Wouldn't they have had to turn information of mental illness over during discovery?" Tom wanted to know.

"Ordinarily yes," Sarah replied. "However, they are not pleading diminished capacity. They want not guilty."

"Are you worried?" I asked.

"Not really," Sarah admitted. "I think the jury will see her for who she is."

"Let's not worry until they throw it out there," Tom suggested. "If they do, Macy and I will be right on it."

"Thanks, I knew I could count on you," Sarah smiled and unlocked the door.

I handed her the report on our interview with Jeremy Blackburn. "We have found you another victim," I told her.

As we walked out of the building, Sarah headed to her office. Tom said, "Let's grab an early lunch."

"Sounds good to me," I agreed and followed him as he headed toward Dollie's Deli.

We ordered without even looking at the menu. The waitress brought our drinks and we settled in.

"Feeling a little less nervous?" Tom wanted to know.

"Yes and no," I replied. "What would cause an eleven or twelve year old to have a breakdown?"

"Do you think it's going to be an issue?"

I gave it some thought before answering, "I really don't know, but it gives me something else to think about."

"You mean something besides Eli," Tom said smiling.

I laughed because I had not thought about Eli all morning. "Thanks I needed to laugh."

"Anything to help a friend," Tom did a mock bow. "Tell me about this restaurant he owns."

"Wow, it's amazing," I answered remembering our dinner there. "It's very rustic with a subtle hint of glamour. The food is to die for and the dining rooms are private with gardens to walk in."

"Maybe I should take Shannon," he suggested.

"Oh, you definitely should. I'll even come babysit," I told him.

Tom smiled as the waitress set our food in front of us, "I'm going to hold you to it."

Smiling I dug into my chicken salad sandwich. Lunch was over too quickly.

WE WALKED BACK to the courthouse. Arriving twenty minutes early, we found a court clerk waiting for us. "Ms. Stephens wants you directly behind the prosecutor's table."

"Did she say why?" I asked.

He shook his head and said, "No," at the same time.

"Okay, thanks," Tom told him.

We found seats behind the prosecutor's table and sat down to wait for people to enter. Then as if reading my thoughts, Tom quietly whispered, "There is a kind of reverence in this room."

I nodded in agreement. *There was something almost sacred in this room. Justice was meted out to those who offended. The victims were given some peace of mind. Or at least I hoped they were.*

We watched as people began entering the court room. Mr. and Mrs. Patton sat in the row behind the defense table. Mrs. Patton obviously distraught kept dabbing a hankie to her eyes. Mr. Patton sat ramrod straight and kept his eyes focused on something ahead of him. Barney Bradford made his way to the defense table.

Chelsie was brought in. She was dressed demurely in spite of the handcuffs on her wrists. Her mother openly sobbed. *It was going to be interesting to see if she had an attitude change as well.* She did not even look at her parents as she took her seat beside her attorney. The officer released her hands from the cuffs and moved to the side of the room.

Sarah made her appearance then. I knew she had entered because of the buzz from the back of the room. She was dressed in the navy blue suit she had worn this morning. She placed her brief case on the table and proceeded to take files out and set them in the order she would use them. She turned to shake hands with Barney Bradford, and then seated herself.

The bailiff entered and proclaimed, "All rise for the Honorable Judge Elizabeth Allen."

The judge seated herself, told us to be seated and ordered the jury brought in. After they were seated the judge said to Sarah, "Ms. Stephens, call your next witness please."

Rising Sarah said, "The state calls Duncan O'Brian to the stand."

I found myself wanting to giggle as I watched the pompous little man walk to the witness box. This was going to be interesting. He was sworn in and the questioning began.

"Please state your name and occupation for the record," Sarah instructed.

"Duncan O'Brian I am the principal at Rivers Edge High School," he said succinctly.

"When did you become aware of the bullying issue at the high school?" Sarah asked.

"It came to my attention when two officers came to question my staff and some students," he answered looking at the jury to see if they were impressed.

"There had been no previous complaints by students?" hammered Sarah.

"Nothing, I would have considered more than harmless teasing."

"Are you aware of the district's bullying policy?" she wanted to know.

"Of course, I am," he replied bristling.

"At what point does it go into effect?"

He looked at her as if she had lost her mind, "I goes into effect the day school starts and remains in effect until the school year ends."

Sarah came back at him with, "Then why hasn't it been followed by you and your staff?"

O'Brian sputtered for a moment, then said, "It has been followed by the letter."

"Mr. O'Brian, if it had been followed to the letter, do you really think a young girl would be lying in a hospital bed fighting for her life?" Sarah asked.

"I cannot account for what students do on their own time," he told her with all the arrogance he could muster.

"Mr. O'Brian, have you seen this photo? Marked state exhibit A," she asked handing him the photo of Michelle.

He became flustered and quickly handed the photo back. Sarah took it to the jury to pass around and repeated, "Have you seen this photo before?"

"Of course, I haven't," he almost shouted.

Sarah looked at him as though he'd sprouted horns, "This photo showed up on every student computer in your high school and on several hundred cell phones, and yet you want us to believe you've never seen it?"

"Objection, asked and answered," Bradford said from the defense table.

"Overruled, I want to hear this answer," Judge Allen said.

"I don't use the student computers, why would I know about it?" O'Brian asked.

"Are you aware this is not the first time photos of this type have been passed around at the high school?" Sarah wanted to know.

"Kids have been passing risqué photos around since I was a lad. It's harmless fun."

"This harmless fun as you call it has caused one girl's death, one girls attempted suicide, and one girl to be mentally fragile as the result of a failed suicide attempt. I hardly think that's harmless, do you?" demanded Sarah.

"No one wants to see students harmed."

"No further questions," Sarah said turning from the man in disgust.

"Cross examine?" the judge asked.

"Yes, you Honor. Mr. O'Brian, how many students attend Rivers Edge High?" he began.

"Approximately five hundred and twenty-five," Mr. O'Brian answered feeling back in his comfort zone.

"Do you know each and every one of them?" Bradford asked.

"I know most of them. The newer students are the ones I am least likely to know."

"Are the students aware of the school bullying policy?"

"They are to go over the handbook and building policies in homeroom with their teachers. These are sent home and require a parent and student signature be returned with in the first two weeks of the year," O'Brian said proud of the way he was doing *his* job.

Bradford asked, "Do you check to see if the homeroom teachers are covering all the policies?"

"I don't check every teacher. I drop into as many rooms as time permits."

"Thank you, Mr. O'Brian, I have no further questions." Bradford returned to his seat.

"You may step down," said the judge. "Please call your next witness."

As O' Brian waddled back to sit in the gallery, Sarah stood and said, "The state calls Mrs. Wharton."

Mrs. Wharton approached the stand and was sworn in. She looked ill at ease in the witness box. *I could muster up no sympathy for this woman who had fallen down on the job.*

"Please state your name and occupation for the record," Sarah began.

"Edith Wharton, I'm a counselor at Rivers Edge High School."

"Mrs. Wharton, were you ever approached by any of the following girls about issues of bullying; Mary Golden, Tansy Taylor, Alana Grey, or Michelle Watson?" Sarah asked politely.

"Each of those girls was in my office once," she replied.

"And did you follow the bullying procedure set up by the school district?"

Mrs. Wharton was taken aback, "I saw no need to begin a bullying investigation over what was obviously typical teenage drama."

"How is it you were able to determine it was teenage drama?" Sarah questioned?

"None of them ever came back a second time," Mrs. Wharton stated as if it were enough.

Sarah was angry now, "Did you alert any teachers to be aware there might be issues?"

"I told you there was no reason to do so," Mrs. Wharton was becoming indignant.

Sarah came back with, "Were you surprised that Chelsie Patton's name came up with each one of these girls?"

Mrs. Wharton let out a nervous chuckle, "I've seen jealousy in the past. Chelsie gets a lot of attention and the other girls don't like it."

"You are not trying to tell me you think the girls made this all up are you?" Sarah was close to ballistic.

"Well, no certainly not," Mrs. Wharton stammered. "I do think it was just the things girls do."

Sarah started, "The things girls do," then paused. Finally she asked, "And those things would be to drive other girls to attempt suicide. This is okay with you?"

"Oh, my heavens, no," Mrs. Wharton sounded shocked.

"No further questions."

The judge looked at Bradford and said, "Your witness."

Bradford rose smiling and said, "Good morning, Mrs. Wharton."

She hesitated then said, "Good morning."

"How many years have you been a counselor?"

She smiled, "Going on twenty-eight."

"In all your years as a counselor, do children being bullied come back to you for more help?"

"Usually I see some children two or three times before we get things worked out," she told him.

Bradford nodded as if letting her know she'd given the correct answer, "Based on your experience, have there ever been any children bullied who didn't seek more help?"

"I don't have any data, but I'm sure there are times when children don't come back for whatever reason," she said.

"Mrs. Wharton, how many children have attempted suicide in all your years at the high school?" Bradford asked.

"Until now, I hadn't heard of any," Mrs. Wharton said, although she seemed somewhat confused.

Bradford pounced, "Would it surprise you to know that in your nearly twenty-eight years as counselor, there have been at least fifty attempted suicides?"

"There is no way, I would have known something like that," Mrs. Wharton was shocked and indignant.

"The national statistics say that fourteen percent of students who are bullied attempt suicide," Bradford told her. "I'm sure you cannot be held accountable for every one of them. So, tell me how do you go about preventing them?"

Mrs. Wharton was obviously thrown by the question. Before she could form an answer Bradford said, "I have no more questions for this witness," and walked away.

"You may step down," Judge Allen told her.

Mrs. Wharton stepped down, still thinking about how to answer the last question. As she did Sarah said, "The state calls Mrs. Kelley."

Mrs. Kelley walked straight to the stand and was sworn in. As soon as she was seated Sarah began, "Please state your name and occupation for the record."

Mrs. Andrea Kelley, I am the physical education teacher for girls at Rivers Edge High School."

"Mrs. Kelley, were you aware of bullying going on at the high school?"

She nodded affirmatively and said, "I knew something was going on."

Sarah asked, "What did you do about it?"

"I followed procedure and consulted with Mrs. Wharton our school counselor," she answered.

"And what was the result?"

Mrs. Kelley looked at the jury, "Nothing seemed to happen so I talked with a couple of Michelle's other teachers and we tried to monitor more closely to see if we could find out what was going on."

"What did you learn?"

"We learned the girls behind Michelle's torment were sneaky," she started. "We could never catch them doing anything, but we knew things were happening."

Sarah looked at her, "What was the next step in your procedure manual?"

Mrs. Kelley hung her head, "I should have alerted Mr. O'Brian, but I didn't feel I had anything substantial I could prove."

"So, you didn't follow procedure?"

"I was trying to gather proof so we could take the procedure through to full discipline," she explained. "I really didn't know what to do."

"Thank you, Mrs. Kelley, no further questions."

"Mr. Bradford," said the judge, "Can you get this done before dinner?"

"Yes, you Honor. Mrs. Kelley, how long did you know something was going on?"

Mrs. Kelley blanched at the question, "I knew for at least three weeks."

"Did you at any time call Michelle's mother?"

"Only once and only to ask for a second set of clothing to be left in my office for Michelle," she answered.

I could see her trying to hunch down in the chair as if making herself smaller would make him stop asking questions.

Bradford was not letting up, "You knew she would need a second set of clothing, but you didn't discuss what was going on with her mother?"

Again it looked as though she hung her head, "I thought we'd be able to solve the problem. We were trying to do something."

"Thank you, Mrs. Kelley." Bradford walked away.

"You may step down," Judge Allen said, "Court is adjourned until tomorrow morning."

The bailiff said, "All rise." We stood as the judge left the courtroom. The jury was led out and people began filing out.

I almost felt sorry for Mrs. Kelley. She had made a small attempt to do the right thing, but had not followed the guidelines set up to deal with bullies.

Tom and I left the court house together. He was more subdued than when we had first arrived. I was too wrapped in my own thoughts to worry about him. At the station I took care of the papers on my desk and then headed for home.

I had forgotten Eli was making dinner. Tonight I just wanted to be alone to think about today's testimony. *To go over the case in my mind, did we have all we needed for a conviction? Was our evidence of past crimes going to be allowed? And most importantly did today's witnesses show clearly they were part of the problem and not part of the solution? Would they see it for themselves and work to change?*

I knew Eli sensed something was wrong when he asked, "Would you rather I didn't stay for dinner?"

Looking at him and seeing the concern on his face I answered, "No, stay for dinner, I just need it to be a dinner only evening."

"Do you want to talk about it?" he asked.

"I really don't," I told him honestly. "It's just this case is taking its toll on me. I need a little space."

He kissed my forehead gently as he put the bar-b-que ribs in front of me and handed me an extra napkin. "I understand."

We ate in a companionable silence. Eli picked up our dishes and added them to the dishwasher then started it. He was running water to do the pans when I said, "Leave them. It will give me something to do."

Turning to me he asked, "Are you sure?"

I nodded yes. He dried his hands and came to kiss me good-night. I could barely breathe when he was done kissing me.

After he left, I changed into my oldest pair of sweats and finished the dishes. I did a work out then headed to bed knowing I'd be awake for a while just thinking. *I went over the day in my head. Why did I feel like I was missing something? I don't even know when sleep overtook me.*

CHAPTER
TWENTY-SEVEN

Wednesday

Again I was at the station early. This morning I was looking through my notes for whatever it was niggling in my brain. Tom set a cup of tea on my desk.

"What are you looking for?" he asked.

I took a sip of the tea and answered, "I'm not sure, something is playing at the back of mind. I just want to be sure we didn't miss anything."

"Let it go for now, Macy," Tom said. "We need to head for the court house and maybe while we're there you'll remember."

Thinking he might be right I grabbed my gear and we walked to the court house. The same precautions are taken every time we come, yet I don't feel any safer, or maybe I just take my safety for granted when I am here.

We took our seats behind the prosecution table. I watched as people entered. I was surprised to see Mrs. Kelley had returned today. She nodded when she saw me look her direction. *Well, at least one of them is interested in how this all turns out. And I don't find myself surprised at which one. I wonder if they had any training in how to handle bullies or if they were just handed a booklet and told to read it. Might be something to ask at a later date, it's not an issue for the trial.*

When everyone was seated the bailiff said, "All rise for the Honorable Judge Elizabeth Allen."

Judge Allen had entered and was seated. "Be seated," she said then, "Please bring in the jury."

Once the jury was seated the judge turned to Sarah, "Ms. Stephens, please call the next witness."

Sarah called her next witness, "State calls Alana Gray to the stand."

I glanced at Chelsie to see her reaction. I was surprised, she looked straight ahead. It was as if she thought she could ignore the jury and things would be okay.

Alana held her head high as she walked toward the witness stand. She was sworn in and asked to state her name.

"Alana Gray," she said simply.

"Miss Gray, are you acquainted with the defendant, Chelsie Patton?"

"I know her."

"Can you please tell the court how you know her," Sarah prompted.

"We went to Rivers Edge High School together," Alana said without emotion.

"Are you still classmates?"

"No, I am home schooled," Alana answered.

"What prompted you to be home schooled?"

Alana hesitated then looked at the jury, "Chelsie and her friends made my life at school miserable."

"How did they do so?"

"Objection, asks the witness to speculate."

"I believe she can tell us what happened to her," Sarah responded.

"Overruled," Judge Allen said, "You may answer the question."

"At first they knocked books out of my hand or knocked over my lunch," Alana said.

"Then what happened?"

"They created a website and photoshopped my picture onto the bodies of naked women," Alana blushed as she spoke.

"Did you speak to anyone at the school about it?" Sarah asked.

Alana looked at Sarah and back at the jury, "Yes and the harassment got worse."

"How did it get worse?"

"I started getting phone calls at all hours of the night from boys and men who," she paused, "they said awful things to me. They claimed I was trying to sell myself."

"When did the harassment stop?"

Alana looked at the jury measuring her answer, "When I left school and stopped dating Matt Alexander."

"Was Matt Alexander a part of the harassment?"

"No," was all Alana said.

"Thank you, Miss Gray. No further questions."

As Sarah seated herself, Barney Bradford rose and buttoned his suit coat.

"Miss Gray, you would have us believe Miss Patton was behind all this, why?"

"She believed Matt Alexander was her boyfriend," Alana answered.

"So, she was trying to hold on to her boyfriend correct?" he asked.

"I suppose she thought so."

"Did you know Miss Patton was dating the young man when you went out with him?"

"No."

"Come on, Miss Gray, no one told you he was Chelsie's boyfriend?"

"A couple of her girlfriends told me after we went out," Alana admitted.

"And you continued to see the young man?"

"He told me Chelsie was not his girlfriend."

"And you believed him? Is it not possible he was playing you against each other?"

"You don't know Matt," Alana started.

"Just answer the question. Could he have been playing you against each other?"

"No," Alana said firmly.

"Do you have evidence to show my client was behind the website?"

"No."

"Then all this is girl drama to get back at my client," Bradford stated.

"Objection."

"Sustained, move on Mr. Bradford," the judge said.

"Just one last question, why are you here?"

"To tell what Chelsie did." Alana answered.

"No further questions." Bradford returned to his seat.

"Redirect, your Honor,"

The judge nodded.

"Alana, how do you know it was Chelsie behind what happened to you?

"Her friends told me if I didn't break up with Matt, Chelsie would see my life was ruined. The next thing I knew there was this awful website about me," Alana answered.

"Thank you." Sarah turned to walk back to her seat.

"You may step down, Miss Gray," the judge told her.

Alana stepped down and I could see the smug look on Chelsie's face. She felt they had won points. I quickly looked at the jury. Chelsie's look did not go unnoticed.

Alana took a seat in the audience next to her mother as Sarah called her next witness, "The state calls Matt Alexander."

Matt came in and was sworn in.

"Please state your name for the record."

"Matthew Alexander."

"Are you Chelsie Patton's boyfriend?" Sarah hit hard right off the bat.

"No, I am not."

Chelsie's face fell from adoration to despair.

"Why does she think you are?"

"I have no idea," Matt answered. "I took her to a dance when we were in junior high. She's not my type."

"Would you elaborate, please?" Sarah asked.

He looked at the jury, "She is too stuck on herself and believes because she is a Patton everyone else is beneath her."

I was enjoying watching Chelsie's face become a mottled red. I wondered how long she would sit there and listen to Matt put her down.

"Were you dating Alana Gray?"

"Yes."

"What happened while you were dating?"

"Friends of Chelsie's would knock her lunch or her books to the floor. If my friends and I helped her, it seemed like things would escalate."

"Objection, conjecture."

"Overruled.

"How did they escalate?"

"I would find Alana crying at her locker because someone had taped nasty photos to it.

"What kind of nasty photos?"

"They put Alana's head on bodies of women in suggestive positions," he blushed as he answered. "Then there was the website Alana supposedly had."

"What happened next?"

"Alana disappeared," Matt hung his head. "I didn't know where she was and she didn't answer my phone calls anymore."

"Thank you." Sarah returned to her seat.

Bradford pounced, "You claim Chelsie was not your girlfriend, correct?"

"Yes."

"Why did she think she was?"

"I have no idea. You'd have to ask her."

"I'm asking you. Did you lead her on?"

"No way," Matt said looking at him. "I told her on several occasions I was not interested in her."

"Did you call her?"

"No."

"Send her text messages?"

"No."

"So when did you tell her you weren't interested?"

Matt looked exasperated, but he answered calmly, "At my locker when I'd find her waiting there. On the football field when she'd come to see me practice. I just ignored her most of the time."

"Yet she still believed you were her boyfriend. Did you play the two girls against each other?"

"No, I don't like guys who play those games," Matt answered. "I believe you should treat girls with respect."

"And did you treat Chelsie with respect?"

"I did until she became a nuisance," Matt answered. "Then I just treated her like the pest she was."

"Did you ask her to stop bothering Miss Gray?"

"Several times, but she only got worse," Matt answered.

"And you're sure you didn't make her promises?"

"I'm sure."

"No further questions."

"Redirect, your Honor."

Again Judge Allen nodded.

"Matt, is Alana Gray the only girlfriend of yours Chelsie Patton has harassed?" Sarah asked.

"Objection."

"Goes to a pattern your Honor."

"Overruled. You may answer the question."

"No, she drove Mary Golden and Tansy Taylor away," Matt answered. "I don't know where they are and she caused Michelle Watson to attempt suicide."

"Objection, I'd like the last comment stricken."

"Overruled."

"No further questions."

"You may step down," the judge told Matt. "I believe we will recess until nine am tomorrow morning when cooler heads will prevail."

Bradford sputtered as if he wanted to object again. I could see Chelsie was livid. She hissed something to her attorney before she was cuffed and taken away. The jury had been lead out when the gavel fell.

Tom and I just looked at each other. It was early to call the case for the day.

Sarah motioned to us to remain. We did until the courtroom was empty.

"What's going on?" I asked. My curiosity could no longer be contained.

"I'm not sure," Sarah answered. "I think Bradford needs to get himself under control. I just know we're done for the day."

Tom and I walked out with Sarah, then we headed toward the station. "I'm confused," I told him. "Why call the case this early in the day?"

"Got me, the judge must have seen something we didn't," he said. "I for one am going to make the most of it and head home to my family."

"I'm just going to go home," I replied.

On the way home I called Eli, "Patterson."

"Eli, it's Macy," I told him.

"What's wrong?" he asked anxiously.

I laughed and replied, "Nothing court is over for the day. Would you like something other than pizza for dinner?"

He exhaled deeply, "If you want to make something, I'm all for it."

"If I fire up the grill I can put on corn-on-the-cob and throw on either steaks or burgers and toss a salad," I suggested.

"Wow it sounds great! I'll be there right after work," he told me.

"By the way, I love you, too," I said without thinking. "I'll see you when you get home from work."

I hung up without waiting for a response. Then it hit me. *I actually told him I loved him and didn't wait for a response. What was I thinking?* I shook my head and went to the store to buy corn and steaks for dinner.

The steaks had just gone on the grill and the salad was in the fridge waiting for dressing when Eli came through the back door. I heard him and waited on the deck wondering how he was going to react to my sudden announcement. He did not keep me waiting long.

"Hey, gorgeous," he said coming through the sliding door.

I turned and there he stood with a huge bouquet of yellow roses and lily of the valley. I was speechless.

He came over and wrapped me in his arms still holding the flowers. He whispered as he held me, "You have made me so happy."

I was unable to do anything but hold him for fear of doing or saying the wrong thing.

Eli sniffed, "The steaks," he shouted letting me go and picking up the fork to turn them. I took the flowers and went into the house for a vase, overwhelmed he had taken the time to find my favorite flowers. When I came back and set them on the table, Eli had things under control at the grill.

"I'm sorry, I didn't mean to shove you away," he said.

Walking to him I put my arms around his waist, "I'd rather you push me away then have our dinner burn," I told him. "I'll get the salad ready." He kissed the top of my head and I left him grilling as I headed for the kitchen to get the salad ready.

Dinner was a silent affair, both of us lost in our own thoughts. *My words spoken without thought were going to change our relationship. I was not sure I was ready for the change.*

Eli did dishes and I sat with my feet in the hot tub. I was not sure if I wanted to get all the way in or not. I knew I was avoiding Eli and the conversation we had to have.

"Macy," he whispered as he sat down beside me and handed me a glass of wine. "I don't want you to feel uncomfortable."

"I know," I told him. "I didn't even realize what I'd said until it was out. I do love you; I just don't know what I want to do about it."

"Sweetheart, you don't have to do anything," he said. "I told you I'd give you time and I meant it. You have your own demons to battle."

When I looked in his eyes I saw the truth of his words. I knew then as I had not known before, Eli was the man I had been waiting for. "You are too good to me," I told him putting my hand on his cheek.

He leaned into my hand kissing it, "No, I've waited this long to find you. I'll wait as long as you need me to."

"Thank you," I said as I leaned in to kiss him, a kiss starting gently and growing with passion.

"We don't have to change anything. Our jobs keep us busy and we can spend evenings and week-ends together," he said softly. "I am in no rush."

"Eli, I'm confused. This has happened so fast," I worried. "I am not someone who rushes into things."

"Macy, I don't want to rush you," he assured me. "I want us to be sure before we leap into anything. Let's enjoy our time together and not worry about what comes next or when it should be."

"I'm all for waiting," I whispered.

"Now we have settled all the issues between us, let's go inside. I have to go home and you have another day in court tomorrow."

We rose walking hand-in-hand into the house. I took his wine glass and put it with mine on the counter. We walked into the living room where he scooped me into his arms and kissed me as if he would never get another chance. When he released me, he said, "Sleep well my angel."

I let him out the front door and watched him from the window as he drove away. Sleep would not come easy for me tonight.

CHAPTER TWENTY-EIGHT

Thursday

Tom and I arrived at the courthouse early. Sarah was already at the prosecution table.

"Who's up next?" I asked.

"Mr. Golden, then Ellie Wexford," Sarah said. "Ellie has done a video tribute to Tansy we are asking to play for the jury. It shows Tansy before and Tansy now."

"Is Mrs. Golden going to testify?" Tom asked.

"No, she is not up to it," Sarah responded. "The Taylors will both testify. I also have the photos taken of Tansy Taylor."

I was okay with this but asked, "Will Dustin Bell, Katelyn Walker, and Abby Stark be testifying?"

"Oh yes, I want the jury to see just how destructive Chelsie is."

"Good," Tom said.

"My final witness will be Jeremy Blackburn, if we get through our witnesses today, Sarah began, "I suspect the defense will call you both back to the stand."

"Why?" Tom asked.

He waived questioning until a later time."

"Ugh," I said. "Could anything backfire on this case?"

"Nothing I can think of," Sarah assured us. "I just want you ready.

"You got it," Tom answered.

When everyone was seated, the bailiff said, "All rise for the Honorable Judge Elizabeth Allen." We rose as the judge entered. We were seated and the jury was brought in.

"Are we ready to proceed," the judge asked.

Both attorneys answered in unison, "Yes, your Honor."

"Call your first witness, Ms. Stephens," she said.

Sarah stood and said, "The State calls Andrew Goldman."

Mr. Goldman entered and walked to the witness chair where he was sworn in.

"Please state your name for the record."

"Andrew Goldman."

"Mr. Goldman, do you know the defendant, Chelsie Patton?"

"Not by sight."

"Would you please, explain?"

He looked at the jury, then at Chelsie, and back at the jury, "My daughter, Mary, God rest her soul, kept a diary."

Sarah held up Mary's diary and asked, "Is this her diary?"

"Yes, it is."

"Have you read your daughter's diary?"

"Yes, after she died."

"Why did you read it?"

"My wife and I couldn't understand why she had taken her life. We were hoping it would tell us something."

"And did it tell you anything?"

"It told about a girl named Chelsie Patton who tormented my daughter. A girl, who showed no mercy and caused my daughter to take her life." He was indignant.

"Thank you, Mr. Goldman."

Bradford stood up. "Mr. Goldman, I'm sorry for your loss."

Mr. Goldman nodded in acknowledgement.

"Did the diary mention any other girls?"

"A couple, but Chelsie Patton was mentioned the most."

"Did you then determine it was Miss Patton alone who caused your daughter's suicide?"

"I cannot put the blame on any one person," Mr. Goldman began.

"But it's Chelsie Patton you blame, isn't it true?"

"I put the most blame on her, yes."

"Did you go to the police with the diary?"

"Yes."

"Did they begin an investigation?"

"No, they read the diary and returned it," Mr. Goldman said sadly.

"Did they tell you why they weren't going to do anything?"

"Her death was a suicide; they said there was no blame."

"So, you coming here is just to get your digs in at Chelsie Patton?"

"No," Mr. Goldman almost shouted, "I came because my daughter was just the first to be abused by this girl."

"Did Chelsie Patton do physical harm to your daughter?"

"No, her abuse was mental."

"Did you witness this abuse?"

"No."

"Thank you, no further questions." He returned to his seat. Chelsie had barely moved since the proceedings had started.

"Redirect, your Honor," Sarah said rising.

The judge nodded.

"Mr. Goldman, is it true you are here today at the request of the police?"

"Yes."

"Did you come here to get vengeance on Chelsie Patton?"

"No."

"Thank you, I have nothing else."

The judge looked at Mr. Goldman, "You may step down."

I wondered why Sarah had not had Mr. Goldman read an entry or two from Mary's diary.

"Ms. Stephens, your next witness," the judge said.

"The State calls Dustin Bell to the stand."

Dustin was led in a side door in handcuffs. He was wearing prison orange. His cuffs were removed and he was sworn in. The officer escorting him, stepped behind him as he took his seat.

"Please state your name for the record."

"Dustin Bell."

"Mr. Bell, are you acquainted with Chelsie Patton?"

"Yes."

"Can you tell us in what capacity you know Chelsie?"

"We met at school. I did some computer stuff for her."

"Are you in the same grade as Chelsie?"

"No, she is a couple years behind me."

"What type of computer things did you do for her?"

"I set up a fake website and taught her how to photoshop pictures."

"What does it mean to photoshop a picture?"

"You take a person's head and put it on the body of another person."

"What kind of website did you set up for her?"

Dustin looked embarrassed, "Just one porn site."

"How were you paid for your services?"

"At first she'd let me cop a feel, later she sent money with a girlfriend who was going to have sex with me."

"In other words, she served as your pimp?"

He chuckled, "Yeah, I guess so."

Chelsie's face became red. I could not tell if she was embarrassed or just angry. I could see she was clenching her fists under the table.

"Were you sentenced as a result of this?"

"Yes, I'm going to do ten years for being with a minor."

"Thank you. No further questions."

Bradford stood and approached the witness stand.

"Mr. Bell, you are now a convicted felon. Why should we believe you?"

Dustin looked him in the eye, then at the jury, "I don't gain anything by telling the truth. I've already been convicted. I know what I did was wrong, but what Chelsie did was worse."

"Chelsie did not have sex with a minor," Bradford stated.

"No, she just sent a minor to have sex with me," Dustin fired back.

"Mr. Bell, do you want to get even with Chelsie?"

"No, I did wrong. I got to pay."

"Do you think Chelsie needs to pay?"

"Yes, she did worse than me to all those girls."

"No further questions." Bradford waved his hand as if dismissing everything about Dustin Bell.

The officer hooked Dustin's handcuffs back up and escorted him out of the room. Chelsie gave him an evil look as he left. He barely paid any attention to her. I could see something going on with her.

CHAPTER
TWENTY-NINE

Arriving at home, I collected my mail, waved to my neighbors, and changed so I could do a workout. Something about today was nagging me. I thought a workout might help me focus on it.

I was showed and heading for the kitchen when my phone rang, "McVannel."

"Hello, Macy," Eli said into the phone. "How was your day?"

My heart sped up at the sound of his voice. "Pretty routine," I answered. "How was yours?"

"Lots of paperwork this morning and meetings this afternoon," he answered. "Have you made dinner plans?"

"Nope, I just finished a workout" I answered.

"Great," he said. "Would you like to have dinner with me?"

"How dressed up do I have to be?" I hesitated.

"Well," I could hear the laughter in his voice. "I was thinking I'd grill us some burgers and vegetables.

"How soon will you be here?" I asked.

"I'm pulling in right now," he laughed.

Hanging up the phone I went to the door. Sure enough Eli was getting out of his truck carrying a grocery bag. I laughed in spite of myself.

He made his way to the kitchen. Setting the sack on the counter he took me in his arms and kissed me deeply like a man starved for affection.

When he let me go, I took a minute to catch my breath. "Hello, to you too," I answered breathlessly.

"I've waited all day for this," Eli grinned from ear to ear.

"Meaning your day went well?" I asked.

"Eh, it's better now. I've missed you." He started taking things out of the sack as if this were normal. "So, tell me about the trial."

"Good, but I'm concerned," I admitted. "Something is going on with Chelsie and I can't put my finger on it."

"Let's talk about it at dinner. I'm off to start the grill." He was out the door and firing up the grill before I could respond. I continued making salad as he raised the umbrella over the table. "Okay, I'm ready for the burgers," he yelled from outside.

I carried the plate with the burgers and a bowl of mushrooms to the deck. Eli took the plate from me and put them on the grill. "Do you want to grill the zucchini, too?"

"Sure, I'll go get it," I answered turning away.

I found myself caught around the waist before I had taken two steps. "What?' I questioned.

"Nothing, I just wanted to hold you," he whispered in my ear.

Turning around I slid my arms around him. "I like holding you, too, but I'm starved." I kissed him lightly then slipped away toward the kitchen.

Eli gave a hearty laugh and went back to the grill. We spent the evening just enjoying each other's company. It was a pleasant way to forget the stresses of the day.

After dishes, Eli and I took a dip in the hot tub, but by nine o'clock he was out and up to shower. I relaxed thinking how nice this had been. Slowly I left the hot tub, wrapped in a towel and went inside. My phone rang as I heard Eli coming down the stairs.

"McVannel."

"Macy, it's Tom."

"What's up?"

"Sarah Stephens called," he started.

"Is there some kind of crisis?" I asked already dreading what now.

Eli stood watching me with questions in his eyes. I held up one finger to let him know this wouldn't take long.

Tom hesitated, "I guess they moved Chelsie Patton."

"Why would they move her?"

"She's been on house arrest with a tether since this started," Tom started. "Her new attorney thought she should be in a private cell during the trial in case things don't go her way."

"What kind of idiot is he?" I nearly shouted.

"Anyway, general population was not where she was supposed to be and it got a bit rough for her," Tom went on. "They have moved her to a private cell in an empty block of the prison."

"Oh this is not going to be good."

"My thoughts exactly," he agreed. "Can you be in early tomorrow?"

"Sure no problem," I assured him.

"See you then." I hung up shaking my head.

Eli came toward me, "What is it?"

"Bradford thought Chelsie needed a taste of prison life and she got a little roughed up tonight," I told him. "They had to move her to a private cell in an empty block. Probably put her on suicide watch."

He wrapped his arms around me, "What was he thinking?"

I shrugged and snuggled in, then remembered I was still wet. "Let me go change."

He kissed my nose, "I'll wait, but I like you just the way you are."

I laughed and took the steps two at a time. I was back downstairs in less than three minutes dressed in my sweats.

"That's my girl," he said enveloping me in his arms and kissing me thoroughly. *I hated the fact he was going to be leaving soon. I just wasn't ready to commit to more yet.*

"I have to get going," he said letting me go a little.

"Hmm, I know." I answered leaning into him.

"I'll pick you up tomorrow night and you can come to my place."

Pulling back I looked at him. "Are you sure?"

"Of course, I'm sure. Call me when you get out of court and we'll make plans." He kissed me again and I walked him to the door. "I love you, Macy."

I held him in response. "I love you, too. See you tomorrow."

I watched from the door as he drove away. *I loved him. I'd told him and he didn't turn into some kind of monster or disappear. Maybe this would work out yet.*

Turning out the lights I headed up the stairs to toss and turn. Sometime in the night I found peace and a deep dreamless sleep.

CHAPTER THIRTY

Friday

Morning came early, but I was up and ready for the office ahead of time again. Tom was waiting with a cup of tea when I got there.

"How is she?" I asked taking the cup.

"Made it through the night," he answered. "Can't imagine what Bradford was thinking."

"Have you checked in with Sarah?"

"She wants us front row today. I think she's expecting trouble," he said between sips of coffee.

"Let's get going then," I headed to put my empty cup in the break room. Tom followed finishing up his coffee.

We walked to the court house and found seats in the row behind the prosecution table. Again the reverence of the room seemed to help calm me. I watched as people came in. Mrs. Patton was more under control today. Mr. Patton was again ramrod straight. Barney Bradford entered to a flurry of noise from the back. I could see he had brought the press. Chelsie was led in, looking as though she had not slept at all. Her outfit was navy blue skirt, with what looked like a silk blouse, and pale blue sweater. She took her seat and allowed them to take the hand cuffs off her. Sarah came in wearing dove grey. She began her process of setting out files in order of use. As yesterday, she shook hands with Bradford before taking her seat. The jury was ushered in and the bailiff said, "All rise for the Honorable Elizabeth Allen."

We rose as the judge came in. She took her seat and told us to be seated. "Counsel will approach the bench," she began. After some hushed words she said, "Step back." Both attorneys stepped to their seats.

"I have made it clear to both parties photo journalists will not be allowed in these proceeding as minor children are involved Bailiff please escort the press corps out." We waited while film cameras were taken from the courtroom. "If there is a repeat of these shenanigans, I will hold defense in contempt of court. Is *that* clear?"

Bradford stood, "Yes, your Honor."

"Let us begin. Ms. Stephens, please call your first witness."

Standing Sarah said clearly, "The State calls Mrs. Watson."

Mrs. Watson came forward and was sworn in.

"For the record, please state your whole name."

"Margaret Watson."

"Mrs. Watson, are you acquainted with Chelsie Patton?" Sarah asked.

"Only by name," she responded.

"How did you hear about Chelsie?"

"My daughter, Michelle, was having trouble with her at school."

Sarah stepped closer, "Can you tell us what kind of trouble?"

"Objection, here-say."

"Your Honor, Michelle Watson is the reason we learned about Chelsie Patton and her tactics. Michelle is in a rehabilitation center or I would call her to the stand," Sarah defended.

"Overruled, the witness will stick to the facts she knows."

"Michelle complained friends of Chelsie's would knock her lunch and books to the floor."

"Did you talk to anyone at the school?"

"I tried to talk to the principal, but he told me to have Michelle make an appointment with the guidance counselor."

Sarah continued probing, "Did Michelle make the appointment?"

"Yes, she did, but she didn't feel like she was taken seriously."

"What happened to Michelle?"

"One Sunday night while I was at my Bible study, she took some pills."

"When did you learn about this?"

Mrs. Watson dabbed her eyes with a handkerchief. "I found her on the floor when I got home. I called 9-1-1."

"How is Michelle doing?"

"She is conscious, but has to learn to walk and talk again. We don't know about long term brain damage," Mrs. Watson's voice had a catch in it as she spoke the last words.

"Thank you. No further questions."

Bradford spoke solicitously, "I am sorry for your tragedy."

Mrs. Watson nodded but her eyes were wary.

"Was anyone with Michelle when she took the pills?"

"I don't believe so."

"She told you friends of my client knocked her books and lunch out of her hands. Did she tell you what my client did?"

"No, but I suspect she put her friends up to it."

"Were there problems at home, Michelle might have wanted to escape?"

"Absolutely not."

"Isn't it true your husband died a couple of months ago?"

"It is," Mrs. Watson sobbed.

"Could Michelle have wanted to join her father?"

Mrs. Watson became indignant. "How could you ask such a thing? Michelle loved her father, but would not have tried to kill herself to be with him."

"Yet she did try to kill herself."

"Because of the awful picture Chelsie Patton sent to the whole school."

"What picture?"

"The ones the police officers found."

"Have you seen the picture, Mrs. Watson?"

"No, and I don't want to."

"For all we know, there is no such picture," Bradford stated.

"There is or Michelle would not have done this terrible thing."

"No further questions." He turned and walked back to his seat.

Sarah was on her feet as she spoke, "Redirect, your Honor."

"Go ahead."

"Mrs. Watson, how did your husband die?"

"He suffered for over a year with cancer," she said softly.

"And how did Michelle react?"

"She was sad. We talked about it a lot and she felt he was in a better place."

"Thank you. No further questions."

"The witness may step down. We will adjourn for lunch. Court will resume at one o'clock," the judge said as she brought down her gavel.

Chelsie was led from the courtroom and the gallery filed out quickly. Reporters would be filing midday reports. The rest would be grabbing a quick lunch so they could be back on time. Tom and I asked Sarah to join us but she declined. We headed for Dollie's; I was in the mood for brunch. Tom ordered a burger. We ate quickly with little conversation, both of us anticipating something neither of us could put our fingers on.

We arrived early and scoped out the court room looking for something unusual. We did not find anything. Sarah arrived and we told her we had a feeling something was up.

"I have the same feeling," she admitted. "Ellie Wexford is up first after lunch, then Abby Stark and Katelyn Walker. I have called their parents. They will be waiting in the hallway and will not hear previous testimony."

"Okay, we'll just keep an eye out," Tom told her.

"Thanks," Sarah said and turned to her briefcase where she started taking out the files and setting them on the table.

We settled to watch people coming in. The reporters were in the back and drawing pads were out. Mr. and Mrs. Patton took their usual seats. Barney Bradford swaggered in and took his seat. Chelsie was brought in and uncuffed. She began staring ahead shutting out everything around her. Bradford must have given her some direction on how to behave.

The bailiff entered saying, "All rise for the Honorable Judge Elizabeth Allen." Everyone rose as the judge entered and took her seat. She told us to be seated as the jury was brought in.

"Are you ready to proceed, Ms. Stephens?"

"I am your Honor," Sarah said clearly.

"Then call your next witness."

Sarah stood and in a clear voice said, "The state calls Ellie Wexford."

I could see Chelsie blanch as Ellie came forward. The bailiff brought in a large screen and placed it facing the jury.

Ellie was dressed in black jeans, an oversized knit top with a beaded belt around it. For Ellie it was tame. She took the stand and was sworn in.

"Please state your name for the record."

"Ellie Wexford."

"Ellie do you know Chelsie Patton?"

"Yes."

"Can you tell the court how you know Chelsie?"

"We went to school together. A couple years ago she approached me about taking embarrassing photos of different girls."

"And you did this for her?"

"Yes, I took pictures for her. She paid well."

"You know some of your photos were used to hurt others?"

"I didn't at the time, but I do now."

"Why did you take them?"

"My dad was a long haul trucker and he hadn't been home in months. I needed the money for food."

"Did you intend them to be used as pornography?"

"No."

Chelsie started up out of her chair, but Bradford put a hand on her arm. She sat glaring at Ellie.

"Ellie, I understand you have done a video for us."

"Yes, I wanted to show the damage Chelsie did using my photography."

"Your Honor, if we might."

"Go ahead."

"Ellie will you talk us through the video, please?"

"Yes, it opens with Tansy Taylor at her last dance recital. I did not take these photos."

The lights were dimmed and the video began. There was a short clip of a beautiful young woman dancing.

"Next you will see what happened with photos I took and someone photoshopped," Ellie said. "I took the photos of Tansy's head. The body is not my work."

The video showed Tansy's head on the bodies of women in all sorts of lewd positions, including dancing with a pole.

"Finally, you will see Tansy today," Ellie said softly.

The young woman on the screen was ethereal in beauty, her fair skin almost translucent as she flitted gracefully around the room to a tune in her head.

"Thank you, your Honor," Sarah said as the lights came up. "I have no further questions."

As Sarah went to her seat Chelsie exploded. "You are to blame. You took the pictures. I didn't do anything to anyone. They were all jealous of me. They wanted my boyfriend." She was up now and moving with a power of her own toward Ellie.

The bailiff reached her and she shook him off still determined she would reach Ellie.

"Tell them you, bitch, tell them how your father put you in porn movies as a toddler. Tell them you are not a victim. It was all your idea."

As abruptly as she had started Chelsie collapsed. The judge banged the gavel.

"Order, order. Get emergency personnel in here. Bailiff, remove the jury."

Bradford and the Pattons surrounded Chelsie. The bailiff took the jury out. Sarah made her way to Ellie and led her to us. Paramedics arrived and Chelsie started thrashing as if she were having a fit. Tom and I helped the bailiff clear the spectators from the room. Chelsie stopped thrashing and lost conscientiousness. Her mother was swooning. Mr. Bradford got her to a seat and she was given smelling salts. When Chelsie was stabilized they loaded her into an ambulance, an officer going with her. Mr. Bradford told the Patton's he would drive them.

As people disbursed, the judge said to Sarah, "We will adjourn until one o'clock. By then we will have word on Miss Patton."

Sarah packed up her things. Tom went to talk to her. I went to see how Ellie was doing.

"Is she faking this?" Ellie asked.

"I don't think so," I told her. "What do you say Tom and I take you to lunch and then take you home?"

"Sure."

Tom joined us a few minutes later and we told him our plan. Leaving the courthouse the three of us, we went to get a car and headed out of town for lunch.

LUNCH WAS UNEVENTFUL. We had a chance to find out how Ellie was settling in. After we ate we headed back to the courthouse. If the trial continued, Ellie would be back on the stand. Mr. Patton was his ramrod self and Barney Bradford was at his place. There were a few reporters in the back, but even they were subdued. There was a pall hanging over the courtroom. Ellie sat with Tom and me behind the prosecution table.

Sarah came in and put her briefcase on the table. Then she went over to confer with Bradford. She returned to her table, but did not go through her routine of taking out folders.

The jury was brought in and the bailiff said, "All rise for the Honorable Judge Elizabeth Allen."

We rose as Judge Allen entered and took her seat. "Be seated," she said.

"In view of what happened this morning, I have postponed trial until a time when Miss Patton can be with us." She turned to the jury, "I want to thank you for your service. I suspect when this comes back to trial there will be a new jury seated." Turning to the attorneys she addressed Bradford, "You, Mr. Bradford, will keep the District Attorney and myself informed of your client's well-being. I expect weekly reports until we can reschedule."

"Yes, your Honor," he replied.

"We will reschedule when the defendant is well. This court is dismissed."

We all rose as the judge did. There would be no resolution today. Tom and I took Ellie home and went to our respective homes.

Eli found me sitting in the hot tub with a glass of wine. A half empty bottle within arm's reach. He sat down beside me, "I was worried when you didn't answer your phone. I called Tom and he told me what happened in court. Are you okay?"

I looked up at him and began crying. "I don' know," I answered.

"Come on, out of the tub. Let's get you some food and talk about it," he said reaching for me.

I came out of the hot tub and he wrapped me in a towel. "Go shower and put on your sweats. I'll find something for you to eat," he said guiding me toward the house.

Looking at him I said, "I never heard the phone ring."

"It's okay, I found you," he answered.

I went upstairs, took a shower, and put on sweats. When I came back down, Eli had made a salad and had grilled cheese sandwiches ready. We ate silently. He did dishes and I curled up on the sofa. When he was done he brought me a cup of tea and wrapped me in his arms.

"Tell me about it," he whispered.

"There is nothing to tell, Bradford caused Chelsie to have a breakdown," I said. "I wanted this trial to be over and justice to be served. Now it won't happen at least not in a timely manner."

"Losing her mind and being hospitalized is a form of justice," Eli assured me. "She won't be able to hurt anyone else."

"I guess you're right. But it seems so wrong," I confessed.

"You did everything you could and if she is ever well enough to go to court, you will be there doing your job."

"I know," I said feeling disheartened.

Eli continued to just hold me. I don't know when I fell asleep but I awoke to a strange sound. It was Eli's alarm and he was still holding me. I smiled knowing there would be a right time for everything, even us.

ACKNOWLEDGMENTS

There are always too many people to thank.

First, I'm going to start with those who struggled through
the Advance Reader Copies to give me a review.
You have no idea how much difference those reviews make.

Finally, a big thank you to my publisher, BHC Press.
I'm so very glad to have found you.

ABOUT THE AUTHOR

Retired teacher Rebecka Vigus spends her time writing, reading, crocheting, hiking, and swimming. She travels seeking the ideal place to call home. Ms. Vigus has been writing since she was in her pre-teens. Her first book was poetry, *Only a Start and Beyond*. Since then she has penned five, full-length novels, one book for children, several short stories, and even a self-help book for tweens and teens. Ms. Vigus has been listed as a Michigan Author and Illustrator at the State of Michigan website.